Mitch

JUSTICE SERIES BOOK 3

KATHI S. BARTON

World Castle Publishing, LLC
Pensacola, Florida
Copyright © Kathi S. Barton 2015
Hardback ISBN: 9781629893679
Paperback ISBN: 9781629893686
eBook ISBN: 9781629893693
First Edition World Castle Publishing, LLC, December 28, 2015
http://www.worldcastlepublishing.com

Cover: Karen Fuller
Editor: Eric Johnston
Editor: Maxine Bringenberg

Prologue

Vinnie watched his face. She could see that he was pissed off. About what, she had a good idea at the moment, but the way he had come into the room like he owned it made her think it was less about the lawsuit and more about her—a vampire. She'd heard from Gilda, her secretary, that Mr. Riley did not play well with others, and not at all with vampires. Vinnie hoped that that part might have been wrong. Apparently not.

"You're very beautiful." Both of them flushed, and he looked away from her. "But be that as it may, Miss Graham, I will not need your services now or in the future."

"They're not going to go away. And neither will I. There are more than just you in this suit, Mr. Riley. They've named nineteen people in this stupidity. And if only one of you lose to them, they will go after more stupid claims." He turned and looked at her, and Vinnie could see that he was getting madder by the second. "I can go away, leave you to whatever it is you do, but they're going to come at you. And if they can't get it from you, they'll sue Mr. Bennett here."

"They're working on that now." Vinnie glanced at Steele when he spoke, but she watched Mitch. "They contacted my firm this morning, saying that I'm harboring you and they want their money. I'm not entirely sure what they think that means, but I'm sure that their lawyer will explain. I have a meeting with them next week."

"You can't be serious. Why are they going after you?" Vinnie started to tell Mitch why, but he answered his own question. "I see. You're the rich and powerful Steele Bennett, right? Will they go after Addie next? Or her grandmother?"

"I'm sure that they have." Mitch looked at her again. "This isn't going to go away. Newspapers have picked it up. A television crew was at their home just last week, and was showing how much they've suffered because of the way you and the others as children have done them wrong."

"We did them wrong? Do you have any idea what we had to suffer living there? The things that we had to do for a single meal a day?" She said nothing, and Mitch started pacing. The man could say more in one step than most people said in a whole conversation. "I ran away. I was only there for less than a year. And in that time...in that time I was treated with atrocities that would...it was not a safe place for a child, much less a bunch of us."

When Gilda stood up, Vinnie shook her head at her. She knew things too. Things that had happened to this young man that should never have happened to an adult, much less a child. When Gilda sat down, Vinnie looked at Hugo. He nodded once and picked up her briefcase, as well as her coat. If Mitch wouldn't help her, then there was nothing much more she could do to make him. As they made their way to the door, Hugo stepped in front of her when someone or something moved beside her.

"She wants to know if you're related to Mr. Horatio Graham." Vinnie grabbed the back of the chair she was standing next to and nodded at Mitch. "She said that she's glad that you're no longer with him, but she wants to know if you killed him or did he get caught at something?"

"He was staked. About ten years ago." Vinnie looked around and saw no one, but she could feel it. A presence that she'd felt before since coming into this house. "Who's there?"

"She said that it's not important right now. And you should know that you brought her here with you." Mitch sat in the chair across from her and stared at something to her immediate left. "The woman is older, about sixtyish, I'd say. Dark hair and wearing a dress from about the turn of the century. I'd say she's been gone for about fifty years."

Vinnie moved around the chair then and sat down. She could feel Hugo there. He would never leave her, but Gilda was standing back. If this was who she thought it was, then Gilda would be in danger. All of them would be.

"Her name...ask her if she's Millicent. I don't know if I ever knew her last name." Mitch nodded. "I see. And you can speak to her? See her even?"

"I can. You can't, I take it." Vinnie said she couldn't see the dead. "I can. Did you know that before coming here?"

Vinnie stood up. She was slightly dizzy and terrified, but she stood straight now. "I'm sorry to have bothered you, Mr. Riley. I'm sure that without your help, the Bruces will win a suit or two, and that might satisfy them for a while."

"I asked you a question, Miss Graham. Did you know that we were a house of necromancers when you came here?"

She hadn't, and she doubted that she would have come had she known. But as she made her way to the door, nearly running now, she could only think to get away, get her little family away. But Mitch stepped in front of her just as she reached for the door.

Backing away from him, she didn't even look at him as she answered. "I didn't, as a matter of fact. I wish I had known, but I'm guessing that there really isn't any way that you could advertise such a thing and expect people to believe you. I'd very much like to go."

"She's not here right now. Steele sent her away. For now." The relief was profound. And before she realized what was happening, she felt herself being lifted up. Hugo had her. But when she looked into his face, it wasn't that of her bodyguard, but of Mitch Riley.

"Let me down." He held her still, taking her to what she thought was the kitchen. "There is nothing in here that I can use to make me feel better. I'd very much like to be left to go please."

"Hush." Vinnie started to snap at him, but she was sat down on a table and a wet cloth was slapped in her hand. "What does she have over you? It must be big for a badassed vamp like you to get yourself all worked up about."

Vinnie laid the dishtowel on the table and stood up. She was stronger now, more than likely due to being so angry. But when she started to leave the room, Mitch grabbed her by the arm. Vinnie felt her temper snap, and she let her power go.

Chapter 1

Mitch woke but lay very still. He honestly wasn't sure if he had his eyes open or not. Moving his hands to his face, a voice, dark and full of hatred, spoke just to his left.

"It's dark because it's daylight out. We didn't...my lady had no idea what to do with you and she brought you here. So that she could rest." Mitch sat up but said nothing. There wasn't much he could say, really. "You will await her word before I allow you to leave."

"Really? Because the last time I checked, I could come and go as I fucking well pleased." He jumped off of...whatever it was stood about three feet from the floor and was very hard. As he tried to get his bearings, and that was hard enough, he also had to fight waves of nausea and dizziness. "Where am I exactly?"

"Here." He was going to hurt the woman if she didn't lighten up a bit. He asked her for a specific address. "A vampire does not give her address out to people she does not know. And no matter the many times I asked, she didn't tell me who you were."

"Lady, I'm in a dark place here, and I have no idea where I am, how I got here, or what the fuck I need to do to leave. Either let me out of here right now, or I call on a few friends to lead me out. And trust me when I tell you, it will be better for all concerned if I don't have to go that route." She growled low. "Yeah, that'll endear me to you."

Reaching out to the two ghosts that were normally around so much that he wanted to kill them again, he was told that they could not find him. Well, that sucked. Then he asked them to contact Steele and to see what he might know.

"She wishes you to stay until she rises." Mitch didn't even bother answering the woman but moved to what he hoped was the wall. He fell into a bed instead. "Wake her and I will kill you myself."

The woman beneath him was naked. It didn't take any light for him to feel the full breasts in his hands or the firm ass that he cupped in his hand when he'd tried to push himself back up. When the woman spoke again, he told her to shut up. When he didn't hear anything else, he tried his best to tell himself this was a stupid thing he was doing, but he could not resist.

Pulling on the nipple that hardened in his hand, he leaned down and took the hard morsel into his mouth before he changed his mind, even if he could have. But then he felt her fingers, someone's fingers, curl into his hair and pull him closer, and all he could think about was taking more of this woman.

"You will need to stop this or things could go pretty bad for you." The voice was Vinnie's this time and not the shrew that had been ordering him around. He knew that sexy, sultry voice from earlier. But instead of doing as she said, he opened his mouth wider and sucked her into his mouth as he rocked down into her body. "You are going to make me hungry."

Lifting his head, he tried to make out her face but could only see the bright glow of her eyes. "I want you. Why is that?" She said nothing to him. "Tell your jailer to go away and let me show you how hungry I am."

"I will not be taken, not unless you understand what this is going to do to both of us. And you must know why you are in need to fuck me." He did; she was naked, and he was hard as stone. "It's not that, you moron. You're my mate. Do you have any idea what will happen if I let you fuck me? What that will mean for the two of us?"

"I'm not your mate. You're just really needy like I am." He rocked into her again and heard her soft moan, which fueled his need even more. "I want to taste you. I have...I really need to taste every part of you."

"I want you to do that as well. Christ, I need you." He rocked again, thinking that he should be scared, but all he wanted was to feel her wrapped around him as he took her hard. "I'm going to come. And when I do, you're going to be mine. You have to know that. I can't...I won't be able to hold back if you come inside of me."

"I just want to fuck you. That's all I can think about right now, being buried deep inside of you." This time she pulled his mouth to hers and he kissed her. A sharp pain at his tongue had him pulling back, but she held him tighter to her. "Get rid of the woman."

He heard the door open, then close. He didn't know if she had left them or not, but right now, he didn't care. Sitting up on the side of the bed, he unbuckled his pants then pulled them open. Vinnie's hand wrapped around his cock almost as soon as he had freed himself. Her hands were cool, not cold but cool.

"Let me suck you." He lay back, suddenly feeling like a man that was having the best dream in his life. As soon as her mouth took his cock, he knew the real meaning of hot. She moved down his body and to the floor while he lay there riding her mouth.

Christ, he was going to come and he had no idea where they were. And he realized that he didn't really care. So long as she was doing what she was, he thought they could be riding in a runaway train going to the bottom of a ravine.

When she let him go, he sat up. He still couldn't see her, only the light of her eyes, and wondered how much of him she could see. Mitch felt her hands then, touching him all over, his hips, his legs...even his belly and chest. He realized then that he'd lost his clothing. He was naked, and his cock was aching for a release. When she nipped hard at his nipple, he held her in much the same way that she'd held him, letting her suckle at his breast while he cupped her ass to his cock. The heat of her pussy at his cock made him wish she'd move over him, bring her pussy down over him.

"Ride me." She moaned, her pussy moving up and down around his crown as he tried to get her to take him. "Fuck me, Vinnie. Ride me, please."

"I'm hungry." He knew that on some level he should have thought about what she was saying to him, but she slammed herself down hard enough to take his breath away. And when she bit his nipple again, this time giving him an incredible yet brief pain, he held her to him as she suckled hard. "Feed me, Mitch. Please?"

"Yes." He felt her body tighten around him, and he knew that in seconds, less really, he was coming too. Rolling her to her back, he fucked her, his cock pounding her as his body felt ready to release like it never had. "Come for me. I want to feel you come around me."

Her body bowed up from the bed. His body seemed to have a mind of its own, and he bowed as well. When he came, crying out her name as he was pulled back to her, he knew the moment that her teeth sank into his throat that he was going to die. And really, he didn't care right now.

~~~

Vinnie drank deeply of the man. His blood filled her in ways that no one had before. It was rich, full tasting to her, and she felt it all though her body. When she licked the wound closed, his body still fucking hers, she knew that things had gone from bad to worse where this man was concerned. She looked up at him, wondering briefly if she had taken too much, been too greedy, when he let out a long breath, his eyes still closed. Then what they'd done hit her.

"Mother fuck." Tossing him off her, she sat up. Her head spun just a little when she did, but she couldn't sit there any longer. He, of course, did not move, so she stood up, her body humming with her release and his blood. When she began pacing, trying to figure out what the fuck she was going to do now, she realized she was naked and snatched up a shirt that was laying on the floor. Before she even pulled it over her head, she knew that it was his.

"Mother fuck." Saying it again didn't lessen the problem she now faced, but it felt better just saying it. She'd just bonded and mated with her other half. A fucking necromancer. A man that could kill her without a single stick of wood or a bit of sun. He could raise her from her slumber and bring her to her own death.

Getting dressed seemed like the best idea, but he was laying there, his body as naked as hers, with his pants down around his ankles and his tie all askew without a shirt to hold it to. Christ, did he have to be so fucking good looking too? Moving to the bed again, she stared down at him and thought of how he'd made her feel, how he'd brought her so many times that she was sure she was never going to be the same for it.

"Well, that's an understatement. Now there will never be anyone else, will there?" She wanted to kick him. Tear his throat out and drink from him. But she wouldn't do that. Despite the fact that she couldn't harm him, she found that she didn't want to either. Going to her knees in front of him, she licked a path up his cock from his groin to the tip and smiled when he moaned. Taking him into her mouth again, she slid up and down his cock as he grew not just harder, but longer as well.

"Come here." His voice startled her, and she looked up at him. "Is there a light? Christ, I want to see you there, with my cock in your mouth."

Closing her eyes, she willed the light by the computer on. It was dim but bright enough that he could see her. When he sat up, leaning on his elbows, she could see his desire on his face, and it made her wetter just knowing he wanted her again. Moving her mouth off his cock but holding him tightly in her hands, she watched him as his eyes got heavier and heavier as she fisted him.

"I'd love to see you come this way. Your cum shooting from the end of your cock." He moaned and told her he would like that as well. "I'm a vampire, Mitch. Do you have any idea what that means?"

"Yes. You feed from people. Fuck me, baby." She smiled at him, thinking the man was too deep in his pleasure to think, but his next words dispelled that. "You said I was your mate. Does that mean you'll be only feeding from me, fucking me? Because right now, I can see the appeal in that."

"Yes." She stood up and he sat up as well. When he pulled her to him by cupping her ass, her pussy at his mouth, she cried out when he sucked her clit hard then nipped at her. "You and I are going to have to think of a way to make this work. We're not alike, you and I. We're...we're... please, more, Mitch."

"Gladly, and I think we're doing just fine now. If you come now, I'll suck you dry and then fuck you." She began riding his mouth, feeling nearly ready to come when he slid his hand up her leg then into her sheath. "Come for me, Vinnie. Now. Let me have your cream, taste you while you flood my mouth with all that you are."

Her body responded to his command as if he was her master and her the slave. As she screamed, this time not holding back at all, all she could think of was how good it felt to have a man taking her this way. Making her feel for the first time in centuries. When he pulled her forward and tossed her to the bed, she watched him in much the same way he had her when she'd been between his thighs. He took off what was left of his clothing, then reached up and jerked his shirt from her body.

"Nothing between us." She nodded, her pussy soaking the bed beneath her when he took charge like he was. "You want it rough, don't you? I can almost feel your need for me to dominate you."

"You will?" He leaned over and picked up his belt. Again her pussy soaked as he wrapped the buckle part around his hand and nodded. "Are you going to hit me with that? Please?"

"Turn over." She almost didn't make it to her belly before he jerked her ass up and had her knees under her.

Vinnie wanted to turn and look at him, see him there ready to beat her ass with his belt, but she was having too much difficulty trying to control her breathing to chance it. The moment he brought the belt down over her ass, she knew she was going to come and come hard. When the belt came down over her ass again, she released, her body screaming out the climax as if she'd not already come a dozen times.

"No. You don't come until I tell you to." Nodding, she thought if she could speak she'd tell him she wanted the punishment. "You come again and I will stop. Do you understand?"

"Yes." The belt hit her again, and she had to bite her lip or beg him to hit her again. "Yes, master."

This time the belt was rubbed over her ass. The smooth leather made her feel sexy, her body purring for more of whatever he wanted to give her. Then his tongue joined the leather, and she had to put her hand in her mouth so she'd not moan again, scream out she was enjoying what he was doing to her. Christ, he was going to dominate her like no one ever had before.

"Do you have a place to play?" She told him she did not, that it had never come up before. "Then how did you get off? You need it as much as I do. I can come, but not like I do when I have a woman tied up."

"I have no one that...I've never found anyone that could take charge like you do. You...have you ever done this before?" She turned to look at Mitch when the belt stopped moving, and he told her he'd never even thought about it. Nodding, she waited for him to resume his moving over her body before she continued. "There was...there was someone a long time ago, but he...he tired of me. Will you tire of me, Mitch? Will you...will you not like to play games

16

with someone that heals quickly and can kill you with a snap of her fingers?"

The belt hit her ass hard, and she knew he'd drawn blood. The slick feeling of it trickled down her ass to her thigh and his hands rubbed it in. The next time he spoke to her, she knew he was close to her ass, his breaths heating her already hot skin to near scorching.

"I'll never tire of you, Vinnie. I will be with you until the day I die." She knew he wouldn't die, not now, but said nothing to him as yet. "If I lick your wound, will your blood affect me?"

"You'll be able to talk to me. Heal faster. Usually. I'm not sure what a necromancer can do with a vamp's blood." The belt moved down her ass to between her legs. She felt the leather at her pussy, then her clit. Riding the hard material, she nearly missed what he said to her next.

"I'll never hurt you, not unless it's like this." His tongue moved over her already healing wound, and she moaned when his fingers entered her pussy. "You're mine. I don't know what I'm to do with you, how to keep you safe, but you're mine."

She came when he told her to. Then when he slammed his cock into her pussy, pounding her so hard she had to hold onto the bed or fall off, she came three more times, hard, fast punches to her system as he spanked his hand down over her tender ass while he fucked her. And when he came, he slid his fingers into her pussy again and the tightness of it made her come again, this time hard enough she felt swallowed up by it and let the darkness take her.

She knew it was daylight when she woke because her body felt alive. Vinnie looked to the dais, the only thing she could figure out to lay the man on when they'd arrived, and saw it was as empty of him as her bed was. Getting up, she tried to think where he could be and felt the hurt of him leaving her in the area of her heart. Vinnie got up and, stretching, decided it was for the best he was gone. She went to the bathroom and realized he'd used it before leaving her. Vinnie thought about what had happened to them yesterday as she took his towel to the laundry chute. She had touched him.

She was powerful, she knew that. Being a pureblood and as old as she was, she knew more of her magic would be coming to her all the time. Her mother was a great vampire in her own way. Her powers were amazing. Her father too, she supposed, but his were darker than her mother's. His were more...evil, she supposed. There were times when she thought them both...well, not evil, but uncaring about those around them. Especially her.

Then when she'd killed her father, a sanctioned killing by the council because of what he'd been doing to bring attention to their kind, all he had been and would ever be had come to her. She was still trying to figure out everything she had gotten from her sire.

As she washed her body three times, trying her best not to think of the way she'd felt with Mitch touching her, Vinnie wrapped a towel around her body and entered her bedroom. Getting dressed was simple...she just pulled the first thing she touched out of her closet and put it on. Going to the upper levels, she knew she had company the moment she entered her living room and her mom was sitting in her favorite chair.

"I'm going to have to have the locks changed if you keep that up." Her mother laughed but didn't leave her. "I've a lot to do today, Mom, so I have little time to be social. Tell me what it is you want from me and I'll think about seeing that you get it. But like I told you before, don't keep expecting me to bail you out of every little thing."

"You've met him." Vinnie didn't even bother denying it. Her mother would have been able to smell him on her and even know they'd bonded. "Where is he? In the lair still? Or have you had that man of yours, whatever his name is, dispose of him? Mates aren't all that special, you know."

"Hugo, and no I didn't murder him. I don't know where he is." She knew she could find him easily enough, but really, she was too hurt to try and find out. "I really have things to do today. It's almost...what are you doing here anyway?"

"Don't change the subject. I'm here because I did want to talk to you, but this is more important for now. Who is the man? Not a vampire but something else. I can smell panther too, but I don't believe it's him. Maybe he knows one." Vinnie told her she had no idea as she looked over the notes Gilda had left for her on the table. She wondered briefly if her mom had read them, then didn't care. There was nothing of importance there anyway. "Do I know him?"

"Mitch Riley." Her mom asked why the name sounded so familiar. "He was the one my client is suing that I told you about. I went to see him to see if he wanted to settle out of court. The foster parents are suing because he called the authorities on them when he left. I told you about it weeks ago."

"Ah yes, that's the man. He was...well, did you ever figure out how much money you were going to make off this deal? I know you said you were asked to take it, but they're still paying you, right?" Vinnie didn't answer her. What would be the point? If she told her she was being

19

paid, her mother would just ask for money. She was over that crap. "Yes. I remember you telling me that now. Is that boss of yours still wanting you in his bed? Men and sex. That's all they can think about. I remember your father and his habit of jumping me—"

"Mom, we've talked about this." Amber Graham smiled at her and Vinnie turned her back on her mom. "You don't discuss your sex life with me and I don't have to avoid you whenever you come around."

"Yes. But you do know that without sex, you would not even be here. However, I still think I would have had you had there been someone...anyone not your father. But that is neither here nor there, I guess. I have you and he is gone." Her mother sighed heavily. "I just guess I never dreamed it would come to you killing him."

Mom thought she'd killed her father for her, but it had been more of a matter of either kill him or be killed by him. Her father had never been a nice man, and hadn't improved much as he aged and got more powerful. In fact, she was reasonably sure he might have been more of an asshole than all the other assholes she knew combined. But when he'd started leaving bodies lying where he'd drank from them, tearing out their throats rather than just feeding from them, the council had taken a stand. And after several warnings, as well as numerous fines he'd never paid, they'd said he had to die. She was just glad that when it came to them fighting again over money, she'd not been in trouble for finally taking him out.

Her mother asked her again about money. Vinnie told her she wasn't going to give her anymore right now. She, of course, whined about it.

"What will I do for income now that your father is no longer around to get it for me? I have bills piling up and there is no one to care for me now. I don't know why you don't just let me move in here with you. It's not like you don't have plenty of room." Vinnie asked her what happened to the money she'd given her last month, ignoring the demand once again to let her move in. With a wave of her hand, her mother said she'd spent it on her shoes.

"Mother, there was ten grand in that envelope. You can't have spent that much on shoes." She waved her off again without answering. "Well, you're out of luck then. I told you before, I'm not going to keep supporting you. Get a job, make it on your own."

Her mother sat there for several minutes without speaking to her. Vinnie hoped she'd pissed her off enough that she'd leave, but she just sat there. Then when she did speak again, it was not about money, thankfully.

"Did you know there is a man here in this town that can take an old piece of furniture and tell you what its life's history is? I mean, so he says. Margaret said she believes every word he tells her because he knows so much." Vinnie told her mom Margaret still believed in Santa Claus. "She does not, but close. I do think the man is shafting people out of their hard earned money. He charged Margaret seven thousand dollars just to tell her the dent on the side of her husband's desk was made by a musket shot that nearly killed the previous owner, when I know for a fact Margaret herself had hit the stupid thing with her sweeper about a year ago. Stupid woman. But the reason I bring it up is I was thinking with your connections I can get into something like that. You can tell people I have this new talent, and I can make some quick cash before they figure me out."

No and hell no. She wasn't going to use her considerable connections and friends to help her mom become a shyster. And then when she was caught, of course her mom would say it had been her idea and she was behind it all. No way was that happening again.

"He's a necromancer." Vinnie had meant to build up to it, or even talk to her mom about the job that wasn't going to happen. But when she opened her mouth, the fact that Mitch was a necromancer spilled out. Her mom just stared at her for several minutes. "Did you hear me?"

"I did. I was waiting for you to tell me it was a joke." Vinnie shook her head. "All right then, you're going to tell me that he only works for one and isn't one. And that you're going to avoid the family at all costs."

"He's a friend of Steele Bennett's. You know him." Her mom nodded but sat there very still. When she did stand up and started pacing, Vinnie continued. "We met yesterday when I went there to ask him about the lawsuit. He and I touched and the power...I lost control of mine."

"You lost control?" She nodded. "Not possible, my dear. He drew it from you. I would bet he does that to all vampires. Are you even sure he's your mate? Perhaps he's a con, like your father was." Vinnie wanted to point out that she was as well, but didn't.

"No. He's the real thing. I brought him here to make sure he was all right because he was hurt by my magic. And I thought it safer than to leave him with Bennett." Her mom didn't speak but continued to pace. "We've bonded and mated, in case you didn't know that."

"Well, we'll have to figure something out then." She asked her what she meant. "You can't be with a necro, darling. You're a vampire and he's...well, he's what he is. Maybe I can have someone kill him for—"

Vinnie had her mom pinned against the wall so quickly she was shocked to see herself there with her hands around her mother's throat. Her mom didn't move, didn't fight back either, and Vinnie let her down slowly. When she was free, Vinnie watched her mom move to the door and step into the hall. But she turned to look at her when she stopped.

"Does he know of Millicent and your father?" She nodded, then shook her head. "Why does your answer not surprise me? You never were a very smart child, and you've grown into a selfish woman too. He can see them then? And does he know what they are to you? To us?"

"No. I don't think so. Father wasn't there, he told me, and Millicent...I don't know what she said to him. But I don't know if it matters. Mitch is gone too, as I said." Her mom told her he would be back. "I don't think he will. I think...he's not going to want to be with me any more than I want to be with him."

"Don't lie to me, Vinnie. You know how much I hate when you lie to me. It's almost as bad as you cutting me out of funds." Vinnie decided that no matter what was going on in her mother's life from now on, Vinnie was not going to give her anything else. "Try your best to keep away from him until I can figure this out. And I will. Then you're going to owe me. There has to be some way for this to work out so that I don't have to worry about him killing me as you did your father."

When her mom left her, Vinnie sat down. She wasn't really sure what her mom was going to do, but she also knew if she hurt Mitch, Vinnie would end her life as she had her father's. And that had been about as murderous as she'd ever gotten, killing the man that had essentially brought her into this world and then just left her on her own.

Chapter 2

The ghost kept staring at him. Mitch had asked her twice what her problem was, but all she did was stare at him. Finally, in a fit of...whateverness, he moved to the other room to try and work off some of the energy that he'd had since he'd left Vinnie's big mansion. Christ, he had fucked up royally there. He saw Kari coming toward him and tried to smile. When she stopped suddenly and stared at him too, he felt his temper snap.

"What the fuck, Kari? You come here all friendly and have one look at me and.... You're staring at me like I have three heads and, frankly, I'm sick to fucking death of it." She cocked a brow at him, but he ignored it. "We're working. What is it you want? Or do you plan to just go around acting like you—?"

He backed up as far as he could from the big panther that was suddenly standing there. She was one pissed off cat, and it didn't take him being told that to see it. He put his hands up when she growled at him. Steele came around the corner of the house just as she sat down.

25

"You've done this up right. Now she's going to have to be taken home like this. We forgot to pack for such emergencies." Steele laughed. "Of course, it would make her a good deal happier if she could simply tear your throat out. What did you do to piss her off?"

"I didn't do anything to her, she just did this on her own." The cat in front of him snapped her teeth at his groin. "Okay, I might have been a little pissy with her."

"A little?" Steele laughed again, but it was cut off when something pressed him hard against the wall. Mitch looked over at him to see Vinnie with her hands around his throat and his feet dangling about three feet above the floor. Addie was pacing back and forth behind them both, growling and snarling at them. Mitch knew a new kind of fear when Vinnie hissed at Steele, her fangs down and her eyes as red as blood.

"Let him go." When she looked at him, Mitch was worried that she didn't know him or what they'd shared just that morning. Swallowing twice, he tried again. "Please let him go. He didn't do anything wrong. I pissed off his mate and she...well, Kari was going to teach me a very important lesson in not pissing her off when she's bigger and meaner than me when you showed up."

He could tell that she was struggling with it. He'd been a real bastard since he'd gotten home this morning, and it hadn't gotten any better when they'd been called out so soon after he'd gotten there. He wanted to think it was because he was tired, but to be honest it was because he was stressed out about a great many things, and having a mate, a vampire mate, was on the top of his list right now. Vinnie stared at Steele like she was still thinking of killing him.

"Did he frighten you, or was it the cat?" He said that he'd been more pissed than frightened. "Yes. I could feel that too. If I let him down, will he kill me, you think?"

Before he could ask Steele what he'd do, Steele answered Vinnie. "No, I won't do anything to you. You were protecting him and that's fine. I can understand that more than you know." She looked at him, then at the cat as Steele continued. "You're his mate, I'm assuming."

"I am. I don't like it any more than you do, but there is little to nothing I can do about it now." That sort of hurt, but Mitch didn't say anything. "My mom, she's not too thrilled about it either. I think she might be trying to hire someone to kill him. I won't let it happen, but I'm just giving you a heads up in the event she shows up sometime."

She let him down and took a step back. Addie's cat moved toward Steele, but she kept her distance from the vampire. Mitch wasn't sure what the fuck he was supposed to do now. But when Vinnie moved to the shadowed side of the house, he realized how early in the day it was and went to her.

"Are you all right?" She nodded, but he could tell that she was exhausted. Or hurt, maybe both. "Should you be here at all? I mean, out in the sun like this?"

"I didn't really have a choice in the matter, now did I?" He wanted to point out that he'd not either, but didn't. He'd been snapping enough today, and he thought taking that attitude with her might get him a great deal of pain. "What did you do to get yourself in that position anyway?"

"You." She asked him how it had been her fault. "How you say that you don't know what to do with me, and that your mother is finding a hit man to take me out. Kinda hurts, if you want to know the truth. Well, I got news for you. I don't have a clue what I'm supposed to do with you either. Am I...? I don't know. Food and sex for you now? Do we live in that dark place during the day and not go out until night? You would not believe the things that are rolling in my head right now. And when I left you this morning, the thoughts and scenarios just kept getting stranger."

"You could have asked me instead of running away like a wounded child." He felt his temper getting the better of him and took a step back. Then another. "Are you planning to run again? I do hope this is not going to be a trend with us. You getting your pants in a knot and me having to rescue you."

Mitch rushed her. There was no other word for it. Pressing her against the wall with his body, he kissed her hard as he rocked into her heat. As she wrapped herself around him, her arms and legs seemingly becoming a part of him, he cupped her ass and held her to him as he moved his mouth down her throat to her pounding pulse.

"Bite me." He wanted to. Needed to really. But he had no more idea of how to do that than he did how to sprout wings and fly. Looking up at her, he could see her need and feel it as it washed over him. Christ, he wanted to fuck her right now.

"I can't bite you." She nodded, but the facts didn't change that he really wanted to. "You're not going to be easy with this, are you? I mean we've known each other for less than two days and I've had better sex with you than with anyone before. I've become someone that I don't like, and I don't have any idea what I'm doing."

"You're my mate. Do you know what that means to a vampire?" Mitch told her what he knew. "Yes, you'll be my bed partner and my food. I cannot drink from another person unless you give me permission or to save my life. Sex with you will be like it was last night, but more. So yes, it will get better as we grow together. We are together until we die, or someone kills me. And you should also know that you're going to be around for a good deal longer than any of your friends. You're like Hugo, a part of my life now."

"We'll never age, you mean, right? Am I going to look like this forever? By the way, how old are you, Vinnie?" He'd never asked a woman that in his life, and felt his face heat up when she laughed at him. "If you don't want to tell me, then don't."

Mitch pulled from her and watched her as she straightened her clothing. He'd had no idea that she was half undressed and that he'd done that to her. When she looked at him then, he could see that she was calmer, but he wasn't feeling very good.

"You won't age either, like I said. Not even if I'm killed or meet the sun. You'll heal faster too now that you've drank my blood." He started to deny that, but remembered her lovely ass from last night. "I would like for you to be what I am, but I know that will be next to impossible being what you are. I don't...you do realize that people believe that we're dead and that as a necromancer, you are a certain death to me?"

"I won't hurt you." She only looked at his friends as they were talking to ghosts. "Can you see them now? After drinking my blood, can you see what I see?"

"No." He had no idea why, but he thought she was lying. But he didn't call her on it. There were some things that they really had to work out. "I'm seven hundred and forty-seven years old. I know that Steele thinks I'm younger, but it's because I'm a pureblood and we're harder to read on purpose. I can also read your mind, as you can mine. So you should know that I really can't see them. Not at all."

Christ, she was almost thirty times his own age. He leaned back against the wall just as one of the people they were working with walked away from Steele and the others. This work...he really needed his break that was coming up soon.

"In six days I had plans to leave here. I don't...I had no plans of coming back. They don't know that...well, I think a few of them know, but I just don't think I'm cut out for this kind of work." She asked him why. "I don't like myself, much less a bunch of ghosts that never finished whatever it was they were here to do in the first place. I know that's not right for all of them, but I'm tired...exhausted really."

It hadn't always been that way. He'd really enjoyed his working with Steele and the others. But long before that, he'd had a good time helping the few that would come around when he'd been a teenager. It was a way for him to escape his life, the horrors of it, and those that still tried to hurt him. Now...people were greedy and cruel, and he was sick of having to pick up after them.

"You won't be able to do anything else. I don't think that the people you help will be able to let you go." He nodded but said nothing. "I have to go to my clients, the Bruces, and let them know that I can no longer help them. I can't help you either, but I can give whoever you hire my files. It's not ethical, but at this point in my life, I don't care. I need to help you in any way that I can."

Mitch told her that he appreciated any help he could get. In a way, he knew that this thing hanging over his head was what was stressing him out the most. They were suing him for a great deal of money, and if they won, which he didn't doubt that they would, his name would be shit for the rest of his life. Changing the subject as he normally did when someone brought it up, he looked at the woman he'd be spending the rest of his life with.

"That day at the house. What happened to us...to me?" She didn't answer him, and he really looked at her. "Something passed between us. It was...it was powerful and painful."

"I told my mom that I'd lost control of my magic. She no more believed me than I did when I said it. To be honest with you, I'm not really sure what happened. I meant only to touch you, and my power really did get away from me for a split second. Where it went, what it did, I don't have a clue. I only know that we were both affected by it. I barely got you to my house before I had to rest."

"Did you know who I was to you before that happened?" She told him that she'd not, not until she touched him. "So now what do we do, Vinnie? You're a night person, I'm a day guy. We have different lifestyles and eating habits."

She laughed with him. "I don't know. I really don't. I have to go and talk with my grandmother and see what she knows. I trust her answers more than I ever would my mother's. And she won't try to hurt you either." Mitch started to ask her how old she was, but decided he wasn't sure he really wanted to know. Instead, he asked her when she could do that. "She's coming to town in a couple of days. Mom told her I'd found my mate and she's come to measure you up. That or tell you off. I don't know what Mom told her."

"She doesn't like me overly much, I guess, or what I am." Vinnie didn't answer him, but he could see the worry on her face. "Just let me know. Like I said, this court thing is coming up and...well, if I have to leave, then I'd like to know that I don't have to keep looking over my shoulder for the rest of my long life."

When she left him to go back and rest, he stood where he was to think. He'd been doing too much of that already, he knew that. But things were spiraling out of control, and he had no idea how to slow them, much less ask to be let off at the next stop. If there was one. When the ghost came to stand next to him, Mitch waited for her to speak, knowing full well she could if she wanted to. It was the same woman he'd been fighting with earlier.

When she pointed to the house, he looked that way and watched the two men going in and out of it. They were dead as well, and even from this distance he could tell they were confused. Mitch looked at Steele when he stood beside him.

"Something's going on here. This is a weird haunting, or whatever it is. These people have been gone for a while, and they're acting as if they only just died. Why is that, do you think? There are four men and three women here, including the one you were trying to work with. None of them seem to know what is going on, and even less about what happened to kill them. This is one of the strangest things we've done, and that's saying a great deal." Mitch nodded, watching the woman as she stood there, waiting for something, he supposed. "She wants you to go and find something, buddy. Perhaps we should—"

"Her mom hates me. Well, not me, but the fact that I'm a necromancer. And she's going to do something to get us apart." Steele said nothing, but Mitch just needed him to be there for a minute so wasn't upset. "I don't know if I love this woman or not, and I have no idea what to think of her being a vampire and me, what I am, but...well, I like the idea that we're together. Does that make any sense whatsoever? Because I have to tell you something, it doesn't to me."

"Then tell them to back the fuck off. It doesn't matter what they want or think, so long as you're happy." Mitch looked at Steele now. "You can do it, Mitch. I've seen you tell people to get out of your life before. You even tried with me."

"Yeah, look how well that worked out for me." Steele laughed, and Mitch looked at the woman again. "I'll talk to her. I don't know why she has this thing for me when you and Nick are the heavy workers here."

"Maybe she just loves the way you look, all tousled up and all." Mitch put his hand to his hair and tried to smash it down again. He'd seen himself in the mirror when he'd gone in the house and he was sort of a mess. Like he'd gotten laid recently and had enjoyed it a great deal. "Go and see what she wants. Then later we'll talk about this business with your mother-in-law."

"Yeah. Right." As he moved toward the woman, he thought of his mate. Mate? Who would have thought he'd find someone to love him. Of course, she could kill him with just a bite, but there were worse things to think about.

The woman pointed to the house again, and he nodded. Going into the house, he followed her, without going through the walls, until they were in a room he'd never seen before. He looked at the small dark space and asked her if there was a light. When she pointed again, he walked to it and flipped it on.

"Christ." He looked around the room twice before his mind let him take in what he was seeing. He looked at the woman again. "Is this where you've been? Where you met your death?"

It was a chamber of sorts. Not a house of horrors, because this place was much worse. Someone had set the place up to kill, and to take their time with it. And they had too, if the things on the walls were any indication…body parts, fingers, toes, even a few things he thought were tongues. Knives hung at different points in the room. A chainsaw was sitting on the makeshift counter with blood, old and dried, on the chain.

He looked at her and she pointed again, then moved to a wall that looked like it was just that, a simple wall. But when she moved through it, he walked to it too, careful where he stepped. There was…this place was a playroom of major proportions. But unlike the one he enjoyed, this one had been set up for death and not pleasure. Pulling out his cell, he wasn't surprised to see he had no service. But he did need the others to come and help him. When the woman came back, he told her what he had to do and moved to get the others. But she stopped him again.

"I don't know what you want of me." She pointed to the wall again. "I can't go in there without help. I'm sorry."

She took him. She didn't just move into his body, as had happened to Nick and Steele. This was…well, pretty fucking sickening.

He could feel her pain…not of her death, though from the looks of her it had been pretty tragic, but of her sadness, her missing her family, and of her sorrow of what she could no longer do. Mitch felt his belly churn and had to hang onto the wall before he felt they could move.

He stood still, trying to get his bearings, till she made him move until they got to the wall across from them, and she lifted his hand up. He watched in both fear and fascination as she moved the doorway open after working the mechanism.

There was no way he'd have been able to find this opening without her help. It was buried within the fabric of the wood perfectly. He had no idea how he could tell anyone where he was even if he could reach any of them.

I can help you. Her voice sounded drowsy and full of the promise of sex. His cock hardened painfully with just that sound. *Behave or I'll leave you to...what's going on?*

A woman, a client, is here and she's taken my body, and I have no way of knowing what's going to happen should I go into this room. I...my cell doesn't work. She asked him what he needed. *Can you call out to Steele or one of the others? Let them...I don't know, tell them to come and find me?*

Sort of. I can go to him and tell him what you need. But we've never exchanged blood, so he's not on my network. Can you fight her off? He told her he wasn't even sure how she'd done this to him. *Great. I'm with him now. Try to...try not to piss me off by getting killed, all right?*

He thought that was excellent advice all the way around. As the door opened, he tried to fight the woman who held him, but all it did was make her angry, and that heated her up. His body burned just enough that he finally backed off. No point in hurting himself if the others were coming to help. Moving into the room, it was all Mitch could do not to scream in horror.

Vinnie? Will you please tell him to bring the police? It's bad. She told them they were on their way. *It's...it's bad. Really bad.*

The first thing he could see was the parts. Not car parts but people parts, large body parts that were hanging from hooks and nails all over the room. He supposed that was the wrong name for them, but right now he was straining just to cope. There was a...what was left of a person hanging from what looked like a fishing hook in front of him, the sharp end of it sticking from their neck. Blood was still dripping from the person, and he reached out blindly to hold onto something. That was when the woman left his body.

He dropped to his knees, his entire being simply unable to hold him up any longer. Mitch closed his eyes when he could see the rest of the person that had been hanging up just to his right. The voices behind him had him yelling for them to hang on.

"I want in now, Mitch, or so help me I'm breaking this fucking wall in. Where the fuck are you?" He told Steele to give him a minute. "Mitch? Fuck, fuck, fuck. Mitch?"

As Steele's voice got stronger, he did as well. Staggering to his feet, he more or less fell to where he'd come through the wall, than stepped to it. He slid a little in the stickiness on the floor twice as he tried to get the wall opened. Mitch felt his belly rebel at the thoughts and tried to think of anything else. Even a train wreck would have been less horrid than this was, he thought.

Vinnie came in first.

Mitch didn't have a lot of experience with vampires. Just a few, and that had been to royally piss them off, but he could see right now that Vinnie was not just mad, but she was going to kill someone soon if her fangs down and her eyes red were any indication. As she pulled him into her arms, he heard Steele yelling at someone to get the police.

"He said he wanted to make sure you were all right first." Mitch nodded and stopped. It was too much right now to make his head move like that. "I'm going to help you. Will you take it?"

"Drugs? Alcohol? Anything that will make me pass out for, oh, I don't know, a month or two?" She told him her blood. "No thanks. For now. I'm all right. It was quite a shock to my system." He laughed a little.

"You're hurt, did you know that?" He looked at his arm where she'd lifted it to show him. "Did she do this? Maybe when you came through the doorway?"

"I don't know." But he could see it was a long, deep cut. He'd not felt any pain and didn't really now. He looked up at Drew when he said his name again. "I'm really okay. I am. I don't feel so well after being taken, but I'm okay."

"You look like shit." He was being handled, he just realized. They were all distracting him while the room was being...whatever they did when the police came into a scene they were on. His mind wasn't working properly, and he held onto Vinnie as she stood there with him. When she lifted his arm to her mouth, he watched as she licked along the wound while keeping her eyes focused on his. Then when she moaned, it was all he could do not to pull her to his body and kiss her. Someone said his name behind him and he turned just enough to see the police officer standing there. He didn't want to see the room again.

"Did you touch anything, Mr. Riley?" He had to think a minute before he could answer the officer. He was decidedly pale too, Mitch realized. "The body, did you touch it at any time? Or any of the...the other things, like the blades?"

"No. I did touch that...I'm not sure what it was, but I think a table? I was falling over and I might have grabbed it to keep from hitting the floor." The officer nodded and wrote something in his books. "And I fell to my knees there, as you can see. There were no living people in here when I arrived either. If that was your next question."

"Right. Can you tell us how you got in here?" He started to tell him about the ghost, but looked at Ray, who was standing right behind the officer. His short shake of his head had him telling the man he just found the door and came in. "But you shouldn't have been able to see the doorway to get in here. Not unless someone showed you."

Alarms went off in his head, and when his hand was gripped tighter by Vinnie, he knew she could feel his nervousness as well. When she moved closer to him, Mitch looked over at Drew and spoke directly to him, hoping that he'd understand.

"There was a door if you knew just where to look, as you just said." The officer said something, but Drew was watching them both now. The officer's anger was apparent, his knowledge scary. Mitch thought to make him madder, hoping he'd say something more that would prove what his mind already knew. This was the killer. "I mean, any moron could tell there wasn't any kind of secret to the way it was set up. This place was a piece of cake to find, really."

"No, it was not." Drew took a step back and then moved out of the room as the officer stiffened. Drew was going for the police, the real ones this time. Relief was profound, and the man in front of him was going to be in a world of serious hurt if he tried anything with them all standing there. At least, that's what Mitch was hoping anyway. "You been spying on me, ain't you? Think you got it all worked out, don't you, city boy? Well, you ain't even scratched the surface of my plans."

"You're responsible for all of this?" The officer, or whatever he was, just smiled. "Whoever did this is an amateur, if you want to know the truth of it. I've seen worse. I mean, even last month we had a woman...Steele? You remember that mess we had to go to in Indiana, right?"

If Steele was confused, he didn't show it. Instead, he just nodded and started going on about the worst scene that they'd been on and how a woman had done it. The officer turned to him now, and Mitch tried to push Vinnie back. But she either didn't get that this was the killer or she didn't care. As the noise in the other room got louder, so did Steele and the officer. He knew Steele was masking the sounds of the cops coming to help.

Mitch tried to think around his fear of Vinnie getting hurt, but he was tired still. His body and mind didn't want to work the way he was used to. He'd had no idea that having someone take you that way could be so draining. He looked at Vinnie, and she smiled at him. A thought, nothing to do with what was going on, popped into his head.

"What is Vinnie short for?" She flushed brightly, and he smiled. "Now I have to know. There has to be a story about it as well."

"My name is Victoria, Victoria Alexandra Millicent Graham." He started to ask about the other Millicent, but she continued before he could. "My mother and father were into another one of their separations at that time, and my aunt, my dad's sister, was staying with us. I'm not really sure why because mom and Aunt Millicent rarely get along under normal circumstances. But she was there, and the story goes that had she not been, my mother might have lost me. So mom, in a fit of what she calls pure stupidity, named me after her. I think she regrets it more than I do. And to get my father pissy, Mom started calling me Vinnie. I have no idea why, as she won't tell me."

He might have said something, but both of them were shoved back when the police, the real ones this time, arrived in the room. It was over, the murderer being killed almost as soon as it began.

The fake officer, Jimmy Bob Madison, turned and fired even as the first officer came through the opening. Jimmy

Bob, known to the people he killed as Bob Bobby for some reason, joined those in the afterlife, and they gave him the same treatment he had given them. Mitch was glad when they took his ghost with them when they left the building. His screams were going through his already befuddled mind.

As he and the rest of them finished up the job, making sure the police had all the information they needed to end this, Mitch moved over to where Connie, Steele's grandmother, was standing. She didn't say anything for a long time, and he was content to just be with her. Vinnie had left him again for rest.

"You're going to be hurt." He started to tell Connie he'd been checked out when she continued. "That girl you're seeing, your mate, she's got a person or two with her that is going to hurt you and the others if you don't let her go. I don't know about one of them, but the other—"

"Who? Her father?" She nodded, then shook her head. "This Millicent person then? Are you saying she's in with her brother and out to hurt me?"

"No. Her father is out to kill her, and you'll be hurt by it too. If not killed." She looked at him then, and he could see the fear in her eyes. "He's been gone for some time, and his powers are huge even now. His sister, Millicent the horrible we call her, is...well, different than he is. And from what I can gather, she's much different than she was when she was alive too. It's said they're not even speaking to each other. And that she avoids him as much as she can living here in the same area."

"Do you know why he's after his daughter?" She said she didn't, not for sure. "Can you find out for me? I could ask Vinnie, but...well, I don't want to add any more stress to her right now."

"I think he's after something that Vinnie has. I'm not sure...there is the mother, but she's a little on the weird side too. Have you met her yet? Amber Graham?" He said he'd not, but did mention she was already trying to figure out a way to get him out of the picture. "She might be working with her mate. They were never the most...well, from the things I've been told, they neglected Vinnie more than they cared for her. But I wouldn't trust her as far as you can toss her. I don't know why or if the things I've heard are true, but she's not to be trusted."

When she left him, Mitch stayed where he was. There was so much going on right now, and he was overwhelmed. Just this morning, before leaving to come here, he'd been served papers saying the attorney for the other side had been excused, but the proceedings were going on. He had to get himself a good attorney.

And Mitch decided it was time to talk to Steele and the others. He had an idea Ray knew a lot, but maybe not all of what had happened to Mitch as a kid. And he had a feeling Nick did as well, but again, not all. There were things that had happened to him that he...there was just so much going on he found he wanted to just crawl deep into a cave and never come out again.

Chapter 3

Addie wasn't sure what she was supposed to be doing here, but she watched and waited to see if someone would tell her. She and Kari had come to this house this morning when the men hadn't been back in time to do this job. It had sounded simple enough, and Steele had told them to be extra careful. They were only here to see what the man who had come to the house with Billy had wanted.

"You said he needed us to give his granddaughter something. But you don't know what." Billy nodded and smiled at Kari. "This is not very helpful, in the event you didn't know that."

"He's a good friend to me. Been hanging out at the same stone now for a long while." Billy had been dead for nearly fifty years, but there were times when Addie thought for sure the man had only passed a few days ago, he was so fresh and lively with everything he did or said. She wished all ghosts were like that. "You'll like him, my dear. He's one of the kindest men I know. You'll see when he comes to see us."

"And what is it we're to give her? And if you tell me once more it's a good thing, I'm going to send you back." Billy laughed. It was an empty threat. Kari loved old Billy about as much as she did his grandson Steele. "Why are we here?"

The moment he stiffened, Addie felt her body do the same. Her thinking was, if he was scared or nervous, she'd better be as well. Waiting for something to happen, she told Kari to stand with her. As her friend moved toward her, the man—a large monster of a man—slowly appeared in front of them. His voice boomed into the room with him.

"What are you doing here? You were not invited." She didn't even look at Billy or Kari when the man's voice thundered at her. "Be gone from here."

"Who are you?" Kari asked her who it was, and that was when she realized Kari couldn't see him. "I asked you a question and you have to answer me. What is your name?"

He fought her. She could see how much it was costing him to not answer her. But when he did, she wasn't even sure what the big deal was. Horatio Mower Graham didn't sound like anyone of all that much importance to her. But apparently he was to the otherworld.

There were at least a dozen others there with them now. People she trusted, friends of the other world. She still had trouble calling them ghosts when they were so real to her now. As they circled around Kari, Billy came to stand with her as well. The man, a vampire he told her, just stared at her. Hatred was almost palpable as it came off him. Billy put up his hands as if to ward him off before speaking.

"What are you doing here, Horatio? This is not a house you belong in." The vampire grinned, but she could still see the strain it put on him to be there. "You will be gone from here now."

"I've a reason to be where you are. I have a message for you to give to my little girl. The bitch killed me like I was nothing to her." Billy told Addie that he was Vinnie's father. "You got that right, and that's not the half of it. The kid has no respect for me, none at all. I've been trying to get to her for months now, and she won't have a thing to do with me. Now I'm pissed off. More of an ungrateful brat than I've ever seen, let me tell you. But you're going to take her a message for me; you being a necro, you will do that for me. You tell her I've decided to give her what she gave to me. A child should be more honor bound to their father than to stake them out for the sun. Tell her to let me come to her house and I'll forgive her for doing this to me."

"I'm sure if Vinnie killed you, then she had a good reason." At least Addie hoped so. He roared at her that his daughter's name was Victoria and not that sham of a name her mother called her. "Cool your jets there, buddy, and give me the message. If I think about it when I see her, then I'll tell her. Otherwise, you have until the count of ten to get your fucking ass out of here."

"You've no right to speak to me like I'm nothing. I was a powerful vampire when I was alive. I am a great man in my own right now too." Addie snorted. "You will respect me, human, or I will find you and kill you. If you know anything about me, you'll know that I can do this too."

"Yeah, good luck with that threat. In the event you missed something, you're kind of dead. And all your rights have been burned up, right along with your body. So you are now down to the count of five. Four. Three—"

"Tell her I want what's mine and she had better pay up. As her father, what I want is mine and she'll learn that or else." One of the other ghosts got too close, and he reached out and grabbed it by the throat and shook it until it disappeared. "You will do well to remember that I was great as a vampire, and am greater still as this being."

"So you said before. And she'll know what the hell you're talking about, right?" He grinned, and she could see that his fangs, or what was left of them, were rotted and broken. She wondered if it had happened in the fire that had killed him or if something bigger had gotten the jump on him. She shivered when she thought of whatever might have been bigger. "Be gone from this family and their heirs. Never to return."

With a shove of her hands he disappeared, but not before she heard his laughter. Addie grabbed onto the wall behind her just as Billy walked to the rest of the group of dead. Addie slid down the wall and sat there on the floor with her eyes closed. When Kari said her name, she looked at her.

"What was that?" Addie told her who he was and what he wanted. "So this is the infamous Graham that Steele was telling me about. Apparently this guy is big with the clients he's been working with. And not so much in a good way. He's terrorizing a group of them and bullying them into doing things they don't want to do. I guess he killed some people a while back that got him in trouble with their council."

"Yeah, apparently Vinnie staked him. With the permission of the council, I guess. I wonder if they know what he's up to now." Kari sat down next to her and told her she wasn't sure. "Do you know if this is why we were here?"

"No. Billy went to get his friend to get this finished. I guess from what he said, this Graham guy has been here off and on over the last few weeks giving the little girl that lives here nightmares. But we're here, according to Billy, to give the family some help. I'm not sure what it is, however. But I'm sort of...well, confused why that guy came to you and not his daughter. I mean...can she see him?" Addie told her she didn't think so. "Do you think she will because of what Mitch is, or do you...? I guess I just thought since she was sort of dead she'd be able to see them as well."

"She's not. Dead I mean." They both looked up at Connie when she spoke. "Victoria—that's her real name as you might have guessed—isn't dead. Not like someone who has been converted into a vamp. She's a pureblood. Not a lot of those left from what I understand. And you should meet her grandmother if you want to meet stern and controlling. Not in a bad way, but she's really different. I've been talking to her about what is going on with their family. None of it is very good or comforting."

"How do you know her? Or do we want to know?" Connie looked around the room, and both she and Kari did as well. "This is going to be good, isn't it?"

Connie pinched her lips, but Addie could see a hint of a smile behind it. "She was at a few functions I chaired at one time. It took me longer than I think it should have to realize she wasn't human, but when I did...well, I might have made a slight fool of myself. I do believe there are a few of her friends that talk about it to this day."

"What did you do?" Connie only shook her head at Kari. "Well, I suppose we could just ask Vinnie or her grandmother. By the way, just how old is her grandmother, anyway? I mean, Vinnie is nearly seven hundred and fifty. Her grandmother must be...sheesh, it boggles the mind. But I bet she'll want us to—"

"I wore garlic around my neck to the next few meetings until they told me to stop it or they'd have to let me go. And I mean, like a dozen bulbs of it around my neck so big that it looked like I'd had a growth there all the time. I swear to you, even I thought I smelled really strongly of it, but Alexandra thought it was funny. I have never been so embarrassed...well, I had to make amends, and that wasn't much better." Connie smiled. "Of course, it was a bit of fun too. That Alexandra, she can be very funny when she chooses to. But as loyal as they come as well. She loves her granddaughter with all her heart."

The little girl they were there to see came into the room, accompanied by Billy and the little girl's father. It was true that the young and the mentally ill could see the ghosts. While most of them were harmless, there were a few, like Horatio, that were just evil and would do most anything to harm those that didn't understand. Addie decided she'd talk to Vinnie about her dad and what it was her father wanted from her. But for now, she had a job to do.

"Hello." The little girl looked up at Billy when Addie spoke to her. An older man was there, just behind the little girl, and was looking at her fondly. The grandfather, she'd bet anything. "I'm Addie Stark and this is my friend Kari Bennett. You're Missy Stone, right?"

"Yes. My mommy is in the kitchen, but this is my daddy, Denton. He's an inventor. Mommy won't come in here because she told me not to talk to Grandpa anymore, and she said she wants nothing to do with this. But I want to. She said he's gone and that I can't see him even though I really can." Addie looked up at the man behind the child, then back at Missy. "I love my grandpa very much and miss him all the time. Why can't I talk to him?"

Why indeed, Addie thought. "Most people, like your mom, can't see him anymore. Just very special people can do that. He's here with us now, did you know that?" Missy bent her head back and smiled up at the man behind her. "He loves you very much, and has something for you that might help you, he told us. Something to help your family out."

"I'd rather just have him back. Can we do that?" Addie told her she couldn't. "I guess I can take it then. But I'd really like for him to be here. He was really nice and used to read to me all the time. I miss him making the voices of the stories."

"I'm sure your mom and dad love you as well." Her dad nodded, and Addie moved to the desk in the office. It was old and messy, but Missy's grandda told her to go to the bottom drawer and pull it out. She wasn't really sure that was a good idea, and had the child come and pull it out for them. Reaching deep into the back of the desk, she touched her fingers onto something made of paper. Denton came to stand by when she pulled it free and handed it up to him.

"I've gone over this thing a hundred times. I just wanted to find some part of my dad that I could give to Missy to help her." Addie really wanted this to be good news and was pleasantly surprised when a thick envelope was pulled out of the dark place with Missy's name on it. "That's his handwriting. I'd know his perfect penmanship anywhere."

Denton sat down on the floor beside the big desk, and Missy came to sit on his lap. She watched her dad while she held onto the envelope. When he looked at her, she could see how much he missed his dad as well. When Denton smiled, Addie thought they were going to be all right even if the envelope had nothing more in it than a note telling them that he loved them all very much.

"I guess he's really here. I mean...I had no idea. I wanted to believe he was around but...my wife said it was wrong to encourage Missy to talk to him." He nodded to the envelope as he continued. "Did he tell you what it is? Or what we're supposed to do with it?"

"No. He just wanted her to have it." Addie looked up at the client she'd come to help. As he spoke, she repeated it to his son. "He said he'd had plans to tell you where it was, but got...he wasn't expecting to go so quickly. The accident, he said, really mussed up his plans. Your father said to tell you that you're doing a great job with your child, and he's never been prouder of you than he has been lately."

Denton laughed. "Yeah, the accident messed up my plans too, having him gone like this. I was ready to have him come and help me get my business going, and he up and has a heart attack while driving home from the library." Denton hugged his daughter before he looked around the room to continue. "Dad, if you can hear me, I miss you so much. Every day, every single minute of every day, I find myself wanting to find you to tell you something. Or show you what I've done. Not having you around feels like a hole in my heart and life that will never fill up."

"He said he sees it and misses you as well. And he hears you talking to him. He wishes he could help you, but he thinks that will help." Addie pointed to the envelope. "He left you that so it will keep you in good with the wife. And to help Missy when the time comes."

Missy opened the envelope and money spilled out in her hands. Hundreds of hundred and five hundred dollar bills landed on her lap and around them both. When Mark picked up the folded paper that was with it, he sobbed hard as he read it. Then he looked at her and Kari.

"He said that...my dad said that he'd been saving for a rainy day, and when it pours someday I'm to use this. He goes on to tell me that he didn't rob a bank, which I have to admit I'd not put past him the way he was. He has no idea.... It's been pouring for a few weeks now." Addie knew that. Denton senior was telling Billy that his son and family were about to lose it all. Their power was going to be shut off, as well as the bank was about to foreclose on the house. There was a second folded sheath of papers with the letter. Denton looked it over, then looked up at her. "It's an insurance policy. I don't...do you think this is real?"

"I would say so, but you can check it out. Call the company there and ask them." She looked up at Denton senior when he spoke. "He said that it's real all right, and you're the only person he could leave it to after your mom passed. He said to tell you he's with her now, and she's as proud of you as he is of anything that you ever gave her when you were a child. Even the automatic toast jam spreader you made when you were ten."

Denton laughed again and hugged his daughter. Addie and Kari stood up...it was time for them to go. Denton senior thanked them as well and faded out of the room. But almost as soon as he was gone, he came back and asked her to speak to Denton about something.

"He wants to know if he can come and see Missy and bring her grandmother." Denton cried harder and nodded. "Your dad wants you to know that he's caring for Missy and will, for as long as he can, be there for her. You too, he said. He said he hears you when you speak to him at his grave. Both of them do."

"Oh my God, he's really here, isn't he?" Addie nodded and wiped at the tears on her cheeks. "My dad is here, with us, and I can...tell him yes. Yes, I'll come and talk to him more, and that he must bring Mom to see Missy. I'd really...I'd really love that."

Soon after that they left, cautioning the man to not say the money had been found and that the insurance policy had been buried deep within the desk, and it wasn't until today he'd decided to look. Addie and Kari decided to have lunch as a treat for their morning.

~~~

Horrie hated the meddling necros. If it were up to him, he'd rid the world of them once and for all. In fact, that was his plan. After he got rid of his daughter. And if his wife didn't get on the ball and help him out with that, he was going to take her out as well. He had plans, and she was messing them up royally. Horrie thought of the day he'd been murdered by his bitch of a girl and what he'd done to preserve himself. His wife had been no more help back then than she was now, but he'd found out how Victoria had gotten into his borrowed lair.

Horrie thought back on when he'd been taken too. He'd been in his resting place, deep within the belly of someone else's home. The locks, he knew, were the best and would have taken a great deal more than anything a simple human could have had on his person to get to him. It was why he stole into the house during the day to be safe. He'd just never counted on his whore of a daughter having the combination. He'd even asked his wife how she'd done it, and she'd come up with a story that just made him madder than ever. His daughter was a thief.

"She took my diary that you gave me. The one I had all the important things in that you told me never to forget. I didn't even know she knew where you rested until she told me what she'd done. I told you that you needed to get us a better home. One we could be safe in. So now, while I'm resting in my own bed, she steals in and finds my personal things and done this to you." He'd asked her why she'd let her do such a thing to him. "I had no idea until you were there. The council made me come and watch you. They said it was to teach me to listen when they speak. They said you must pay, and they wanted me to know that you were. They even built this structure for me to stand in so I'd be safe from the sun. But they also warned me that, should I look away, then the shelter would open and I would join you." He'd screamed at her then, telling her that her daughter had had no right to do this to him. As her mate, she could not harm him. "I didn't, Horrie. I was there to do what I was told or join you. Vin...Victoria is the one that did this to us. And her hatred of you makes everything that the laws of the vampire have written down seem like nothing in comparison. They told me that either you die and I watch, or I was to be staked out beside you to die as well. I just couldn't do it. I'm so sorry."

Horrie had been lucky in his death to have been to see this great witch the week before Victoria had caught him. The woman had told him how to keep himself from dying...actually, what she'd told him was that she could keep his mind alive, that his body was going to be shit out of luck. And when his daughter, his own flesh and blood, had staked him out like nothing more than an ant under a magnifying glass, he'd cursed her and had nearly forgotten the spell he'd needed to say to keep his mind awake. What he hadn't counted on was that he'd be nothing more than a ghost with not much in the way of power. But he'd taken care of that as well. The witch, sadly, could teach him no more, as he'd killed her in a fit of rage a few days ago. Horrie looked at the man with him, his only ally in all this, when he spoke.

"They're leaving the house. Can we get in again?" Horrie looked up at the house he'd been at until today, and sneered at the two women that had banished him from his fun. Horrie knew he'd not be able to enter the house, and even if he could the people in it were off-limits to him. The fucking necro had worded things just right for that to be taken from him.

He'd been watching the young woman of the house in the shower earlier in the week when he'd been told another ghost had been snooping around. Today was the first time he'd been able to catch him at it, and now he could no longer go there. Not even to scare the kid, which had been fun too. He glanced over at his familiar, Crocker, and smiled.

"Go with them. Make sure they have something befall them. Could be that one of them can come to my side sooner rather than later." Crocker moved along the sidewalk, but just far enough back so they'd not catch on. Humans, especially human women, were as stupid as dogs as far as Horrie was concerned.

As he made his way to the place where he'd been murdered, he thought about his daughter and her poor life choices that day. Horrie looked at the ground where he'd been staked out, but never got close enough that he could touch the area. Something about it made him feel weird, like he was dying all over again. He remembered her words to him as if she was speaking them to him now.

"You've killed enough, and according to the governing body that watches out for idiots like you, it's time you paid the price for your deeds." He'd told her he'd only just begun. "Do you have any idea what they're going to do once they figure out what has been murdering the women? Do you have a single clue in that thick fucking head of yours what they'll do to the rest of us? How they'll react when they know it's a vampire and we're as real as they are? You motherfucker, you're going to get us all killed."

"You'll keep a civil tongue in your head there, my girly. You've not reached an age where I will not beat you." She laughed. He could see why she'd not taken him seriously with him all spread out on the ground like he'd been. But to have done what she'd done was uncalled for…and to have done it to her own father. "Let me up from this thing and I'll show you how to treat someone."

"No." He hadn't wanted to believe she'd leave him there to die. And when his wife had shown up later in the evening to sit in a chair next to where his daughter had him tied up, he realized he could no longer command her to come free him either.

Horrie was still trying to work out how that had happened. She'd told him later what had happened to her, of course. That they'd made her do it. He had been very pissed then, but now he'd found that he needed his wife living. Without her and her ability to make things happen that he no longer could, he would not be able to carry out his most brilliant plan against his daughter. Horrie remembered looking at his daughter as she stood over him, looking down at his outstretched body like it sickened her to be there.

"And what do you think I've done to you, Victoria? Perhaps you think I should have just tried to live the way I was. Had you just done for me what you should have, given me what I demanded, then perhaps I might not have killed so many people. Why didn't you give me the money when I wanted it? It's not like you didn't have plenty." She just snorted at him. "Answer me, damn it. I'm your father."

"Well, since you seem to not be in any kind of hurry to die out here, let me start with when I was a child. When you killed my nanny. Did you have to murder her in my bed where you'd been fucking her?" He'd done that, yes, but it was his right to do so. He was paying her, was he not? Or at least someone was. He asked Victoria the same thing. But she was on a roll now and would not see his reasons. "Then there was the teacher you decided would be a good fuck. Took her right there on the desk of my classroom—my home room—and left her dead body there for us to find. Why? Why were you even there? It's not like you did anything else for me when it came to school work."

"I went there on your behalf." Victoria asked him what that was for. "I don't know as of this moment. But you cannot expect me to remember that after so many years. I do recall she wasn't that bad of a fuck, however, and her blood tasted as sweet as honey."

His wife had sobbed, and he turned to her. Before he could blame her for his failings, she spoke first. "Horrie, just try to be nice to her. I know she can't let you go, but if the council sees you weren't all bad, maybe they'll let me free you." He snorted at her. "Horrie, please tell them the other women were nothing to you. That...that you loved me and those women lied about you taking them."

"I did take them, you fool. You were not giving me enough, so I had to go elsewhere. And drinking from them was as much fun as it was fucking them." Good, he'd told her. As he jerked on the silver chains again, he ordered Vinnie to come to him and let him loose. "I will not tolerate this sort of behavior, Victoria, nor from you, Amber. I demand that you unchain me before the sun comes up. If it was a lesson you wished to teach me, then sadly you wasted your time. I do not pretend to be anything but what I am. A vampire, from a race of beings so superior to all that I do not abide by their rules."

"Then you can roast in hell."

As Victoria left him, the sun was beginning to rise over the mountain. His wife sat there in her little hut, sobbing hard. He'd not been able to see a sunrise for a very long time, and still wondered why the humans would go to great lengths to see such a sight. When his feet began to burn, the pain so incredible he was nearly sick with it, he began to think his daughter had been delayed or she really wished for him to be hurt. After he felt the burn of his belly, his legs beyond help at that point, he started screaming for her to come back, anyone to come and save him. As the heat began to burn at his chest, he remembered the spell to save himself. He might have waited just a little too long, he thought now.

As the fire on his body began to burn into his face, his eyes no longer working, he began to chant the words that should have saved him. The pain was overwhelming him and the words had been hard to remember, but he worked at it until he could no longer speak. His mouth had...he thought it had fallen from his face even as he began to chant in his head. When he felt his soul, or whatever it was, leave his body, he wanted to find his family and show them he'd won, that he'd beaten them after all. But when he turned to find them, he saw a man standing there smiling.

"Never had me a vamp to bring over before. You surely do look like you've had a time of it. Piss off the little woman, did you?" Horatio asked him what he was talking about. "You. You've been burned to a crisp. That'll fade after a time, but you'll have to get used to the stares between now and then. Thought maybe you'd done gone and.... Well, never mind. What's done is done now. Here you go."

The book, small and full of pages that were colored, he just stared at without taking it. The man told him it was his helpful guide to being dead. Horrie told him he wasn't dead, that he'd prepared for that.

"I'm sure you have, and that's a good thing. But you're dead and this here book will answer your questions. Just don't be losing it. You need to keep that on your person at all times. Don't know for sure what happens to them after a bit, but you keep an eye on it." The man shook the book at him. "You need to take it. It won't work for nobody else but a necro, and you don't want them to get your book."

"I'm not dead. Get away from me." The man and the book had disappeared, and Horrie stood there for several minutes just trying to figure out what he'd have to do now to get himself a body. It took nearly a year for him to realize he *might* should have kept the book and there was no getting a body to replace his own. He was dead. As he tried to rest now knowing he wouldn't, he thought of how he'd gotten to the point where his daughter had gotten to him too.

Chapter 4

Vinnie wasn't sure where she was supposed to go as she made her way to the upper floors of her home. Having the house opened up again was noisy as well as dusty. She thought about having them leave for the night so she could rest, but she really wasn't prepared for her grandmother to be there at the table talking to Hugo. He stood when she entered the big room, but her grandmother only offered her cheek.

"You've been resting poorly, my child." She told her she'd gotten woken up a couple of times. "Would this be the new mate your mother was going on about? I swear to you, Vinnie, that your mother gets something in her head and there is no changing her mind. I should like to meet this man of yours."

"I'm guessing you know what he is." She said she did and wasn't concerned. "Mom thinks he's going to be bringing us up from our resting places and having the sun beat down on us. I don't think that's the way it works."

"It is, as a matter of fact. When I was younger, when there were fewer of us than there are now, we heard stories of a necromancer that would do just that. He'd go from cemetery to cemetery and raise the dead, then put them all to rest again when he'd find some vampires. I was never sure how he did that part, but perhaps we can ask your young man." Vinnie told her he more than likely wouldn't know either. "Yes, I suppose not. I doubt very much that is done anymore. But then, they had less of an understanding than they do now. Some do anyway. Now we're considered sexy. But I still would like to meet him. Does he live here, with you now?"

"No. As a matter of fact, I have no idea where he lives when I'm resting." Vinnie made a mental note to ask Mitch if he wanted to live there. It had been on her mind to ask him yesterday, but she'd forgotten. She'd asked the staff to start airing things out and restocking the upper floors, and she hoped he'd like it there well enough that she'd not have to move. This place was safe for her. "I'll talk to him. So, tell me what Mom wants you to do?"

Her grandmother waved her off, and she knew better than to push the subject. If she wasn't worried, then neither was Vinnie. When Hugo shifted into his animal and lay at her feet, Gilda came in to tell her what things she needed for Vinnie to do tonight, as well as any phone calls she'd not been able to take care of. Which were few, as Gilda knew her job well. After that, it was just the two of them and Hugo.

"So, you've decided not to take that case, the one that brought you to Mitch. I'm so glad to hear that. It's a stupid way for some people to get money if you ask me. Suing people for things that should never have made it to court in the first place." Vinnie agreed. "Did they really think they should continue collecting from the government on children they were being paid to watch when they were no longer there? And now what? They want more? Stupid."

"Yes. And the fact that Mitch had had enough and ran makes me wonder what happened to him. The Bruces said it was a loving and very religious home. They project a nice image of people down on their luck. I have to admit, though, there are things I felt there, but nothing I could put my finger on. Had it not been for my boss begging me to take the case, I wouldn't have even considered it." Her grandmother said her boss was a money grubbing fool anyway, and would sue his own mother if he thought he'd win. "You never did like him, but I think you might be right. And as for the house, I didn't believe that either. There is an odor of drugs and that nasty smell of beer about them. And no matter how many times they brush their teeth, it's in their skin and hair. I think even then I was thinking of leaving the firm. It's...sort of my ticket out by doing it for him."

"Amber says they're suing you now as well." Vinnie wasn't worried about that either. She could pay them ten times what they were asking for and never see a difference in her lifestyle. Vinnie wasn't going to pay them anything, not ever, but she could. She had money, a great deal of it, but had little to no use for it most of the time.

"I have been looking for someone to help you should you need it. And I've sent over Roger, my friend, to help Mitch out. He's going to take the case for him. He said that Mr. Bennett has one for him as well, but I think Richard convinced them he has a great deal more experience in that department. And Roger is a shark when it comes to sniffing out shitty people."

"I have sent over some help too. Not attorneys, mind you, but someone to keep an eye on the couple. They're not very...they really should buy some curtains when this is done." Vinnie laughed with her grandmother. "They have made it easy for the spies I've sent in to check on them."

She thanked her grandmother. "Dad is around. He's been seen with a couple of ghosts, I've heard. Not the kind I'd like to meet up with. And so is Millicent. She's...she has been following me, but she's not harmed me or tried to contact me. I think she's avoiding Dad if you want to know the truth." Her grandmother leaned back in her seat and asked her what he wanted. "He wants me dead, I guess. Not that I blame him all that much, but he didn't get anything didn't deserve. You know that as well as I do. Had he and Mom just had a little more care of what they were doing, he'd still be alive pestering us all."

"No. And the fact you had the backing of the council has made your life easier as well by taking him out the way you did, I would imagine." Vinnie told her it had. "Your mother, she's thinking if she kills off your mate, then things will be all right. I think she's wrong and she's going to end up where your father is. Dead. Did she tell you she wants to move in here? That she thinks you owe her? What you could possibly owe her is beyond me."

"I don't know either, but yes, every time I talk to her I think there is something wrong with her. I mean...." Vinnie got up to pace and tried to think how to talk to her grandmother. "She's been acting a little off lately. Have you seen it?"

"Your mother has always been a little off, Vinnie. You're going to have to be much clearer in what you mean now. Why that woman didn't do something before now about her finances is beyond me. Having money is essential and something you cannot do without. And her mate? It was almost as if she liked what he was doing, killing the humans to get us caught." Vinnie had thought the same thing and had been a little shocked when her mom had nothing. Not even the house she was in was hers. Where the hell had they spent all the money she'd loaned them over the years? Of course Vinnie had never gotten it back, but she did help them a great deal.

"About six months or so ago, she came to me and asked me for the ring you gave me. The diamond one Grandda gave you." Her grandmother sat up high in the chair and asked her if she'd gotten it. "No. I told her I didn't know where it was at that time. And she's since asked me four more times for it. I had Hugo take all the jewelry you gave me, as well as some of the other personal items I've collected over the years, to my vault in the suites where I rest. I never thought I'd have to use it against my own mother when I had it put in, but I thought it would be safer for my things if I wanted to keep them."

"What do you suppose she wants with them? You don't suppose she planned to sell them, do you? I know that she and your father never had a pot to piss in, and I've also been made aware that you've stopped paying their bills too. Good for you, child. They're older than dirt. They need to act like it." She wasn't supporting them anymore, and told her grandmother what she'd found out when she'd checked her finances. "So she's borrowed against a house she doesn't own. How well do you suppose that is going to go over when the owners find out? Not well, I'm sure. I wonder how she even managed that."

"Dad, I'm sure. He can move among the humans now, and I heard he's been whispering in the ears of some bankers. Mom had about ten grand in her account a few weeks ago, and now it's gone too. Plus, I've told her that she won't get anything else from me. Not for any reason." Vinnie sat down on the chair then and picked up Hugo. He was a huge cat and much too big for her to pull onto her lap, but she needed the comfort of him there. She noticed that grandmother's bird was there as well, a large falcon that had been with her for as long as Vinnie could remember. "The witch is gone as well, the one he'd gone to for help just before he was staked out. I tried to tell her he'd be back, but she said she was too powerful for him to mess with."

"Do you suppose he ever found out that she was working with you?" Vinnie told her she didn't think so. "Then you'll have to find her if you can. Unless you already believe her to be dead."

"I do. The connection we had is gone. There is nothing left of her." Running her hand down Hugo's back, she thought of everything that had been bothering her lately about her mom. "I'm going to talk to Mitch too. I think that...I think he'll be safer here than living where he is. I'm guessing you know who he works for and the fortress he has there."

"Yes. And I know someone that you should talk to as well. I don't know if you can speak directly to her, but contact Connie Aster. She's buried out there on the land. Steele is her grandchild." Vinnie had already figured that part out. "Vinnie, take care you don't get caught with Horrie. Your father wasn't a stable man when he was alive. He couldn't be much better as a dead man. And I've heard rumors of his murdering sprees even now."

"Dad will hurt Mitch, won't he?" She told her that he'd kill him, and they both knew it. "I don't...I want you to meet him. When I can...I don't know a great deal about him yet, but I like him a great deal. He's funny, considerate, and he seems to have this sadness about him that I want to fix for him."

"Talk to him, darling." Hugo stiffened in her arms, but then relaxed. Both her and her grandmother looked at the door when Gilda opened it. She shouldn't have been surprised to see Mitch there. But seeing Steele with him had her standing in front of her grandmother. Steele stopped moving and put his hands out in front of him. It was not that she didn't trust him, Vinnie just didn't know him all that well.

"I won't harm either of you. I'm not...please, don't be afraid of me." She nodded but didn't move. Steele laughed a little. "You're going to have to learn to trust me at some point. And I swear to you, I've come to talk to you about good things, not just bad ones."

"Are there bad things you need to tell me?" Steele glanced at Mitch before he nodded. "Then let's start with those. I'd like to end on a good note for a change."

"All right." After the introductions were made, Gilda brought in tea and a plate of cookies. There were four cups, and before Vinnie could ask her who else was coming, Gilda looked at her.

"I wanted them to be comfortable." Vinnie nodded and tried to remember the last time she'd held a cup, much less drank from one. Mitch laughed and she looked at him now.

"Don't do anything you'd not do if we weren't here. You don't drink tea, that's fine." He picked up the plate of cookies and took four before handing it to Steele. "Your father threatened Addie and Kari today. And in doing so, he's pissed the two of them off. Not a good thing if you ask me."

"Did he hurt them?" Her grandmother looked at her when Mitch said that he'd not. "Well then, it seems things are worse than I thought. He apparently knows about your mate. You must do something now, my dear."

"He didn't appear to know about me." They both looked at Mitch when he spoke. "He only had a message for you and told them in no uncertain terms that she was to give it to you. Addie said she and Kari talked it over, and rather than kill him again, they thought they'd see what you wanted to do. But he is coming for you, and I'd say he thinks he's going to win, too, from what they said. I'm assuming the rumors are true and you did have something to do with his death."

"Yes. I did it. With the permission of the council. Father was getting us into trouble with the humans. Killing and leaving bodies in a position that would lead them right to our doorsteps. And if not ours, then some innocent that might not have anything to do with being a vampire." Vinnie put Hugo down and got up to pace. She thought better when she could move, and did so now. Hugo moved to Mitch and put his head on his leg and watched him. Mitch asked her if he could pet him. "I'd say you should let him have your scent. He's my familiar. I know you think only witches have them, but he protects me and my household during the day while I rest. He's as old as I am and as powerful when necessary."

"I know you have to stay in the darkness during the day, and while I'd like to say I can handle protecting you from everything, I know I can't. Also, I have no safe place for you to stay either." Mitch looked around. "I'd say this is about as safe as you can get it, and I'd bet it has doorways and extra things in it that no normal house might have."

"I bought it from a vamp that lost his wife some time ago. He'd built it to protect them both. He sadly wasn't here when the humans came for them. But you're right, it's as safe as I can get it. I've worked with a witch to make sure the house is impregnable too." Steele laughed. "You think I'm lying to you?"

"We got in." She asked him what he meant. "We're not human, and I'm assuming that's what you were guarding against. Right? But you had no ward on this house, other than to keep out mice and bugs. There was a little bit of a spell on the door we passed through, but I think that was more for humans than anything else. If your father wanted in here...well, had he wanted in here before, he would have been able to come in while you rested without any problems. In fact, I think he's been here a great deal since his death. I don't know about the lands beyond this house, but the rest, as of now, is safe."

Vinnie sat down next to her grandmother. "She told me it was safe against all forms of threat. And that as long as I was here, no harm would come to me and mine."

"You've been lied to. I'm really sorry about that, but you are as safe as I can make you now. Which is about the best. I'm not bragging, just wanting you to know you can trust me with this and your life." Steele stood up and moved to the wall just behind her. "There's a wall just here, did you know that? It's the way your father and mother were getting in before and your mother is using now. I don't know what they're doing here...the ghosts that live here haven't said."

The wall moved under his touch, and behind it was a set of stairs. She'd bet anything it led to her rooms under the basement of the house. He reached in and turned on the light, and she could see it had recently been cleaned and no cobwebs were present. Vinnie looked at her grandmother.

"Did you know this was here?" Her grandmother shook her head, shock on her face. "Then who would have cleaned it up? Not my mother for sure. She's never lifted her finger to do a damned thing since I've known her."

"We might be able to help you with that question." Mitch cleared his throat and nodded to the door as he continued. "There is someone here that needs to talk to you, if you'll allow it." She looked at the door and tried to think what he was indicating. Just then, Steele told her to trust him. When he reached out his hand, a man was standing there she'd not seen in decades.

"Luther?" He nodded and looked around the room. "What...? I don't understand. What are you...? I thought you were dead."

"I am. My goodness, but you've done so much to this room." He started to move to the window, but Steele cautioned him that he had to stay close to him. "Sorry. But I've been summoned by Constance Aster...Connie, I guess she goes by now. But she said you might need me for a few things. You know her?"

"No. But my grandmother does." Her grandmother nodded when they turned to her. "What are you doing here? And why would she summon you to come to me now?"

"I know this house better than anyone, as you know. I built it after all, but there are things about it that you should be made aware of. Like this doorway. It does go down to your sublevels, but not to your lair." She nodded, still trying to understand what was going on. "Vinnie, your mother knows about this doorway but not the others. She has been in and out of here, I'm told. When I was contacted by Connie, she said she's had people keeping an eye on it. You have had a couple of visitors that I'm sure you might not want to see."

"You mean my parents?" He nodded. "Can they get into the house from the outside? Am I even safe in my own home?"

"You are now." Luther looked at Steele. "He is a good man, Mr. Bennett. You should trust him above your mother. And this man as well. Mitch Riley is...there is not a better man that you can know than him and the rest of the men who help my kind with justice."

When the man moved her through the house with Steele and Mitch, all she could think about was how her mom was somehow doing this with her dad. Her grandmother had opted out of going to the other doorways, saying she was going to find Connie and talk to her about locating the man who had sold her the home she lived in. Perhaps there were ways to get in and out of it she needed to know about.

After Luther left them, Steele said he needed to get home as well, and Mitch said he'd talk to him later. As they sat on the couch, neither of them talking, Vinnie wondered aloud what she was supposed to do now.

"I'd like to stay here." She nodded, telling him she had planned to talk to him about it anyway. "I don't mean just tonight, but from now on. I could take you back to my place, but it's Steele's home."

"I'd like that as well." She stretched, thinking there could be some benefits of having him there all the time. "I won't need to worry about you, and if you're here you're safe. And we could...I want to ride you while I drink from you."

~~~

Mitch had no idea why the thought of her biting him made him hard as stone. Actually, everything about her made him hard. But all he could think about was he wanted to sink his teeth into her as well. Looking at her now, all he could think of was that he was hers and would be for the rest of their lives. As he stripped down to his bare skin and sat on the couch, he watched her undress for him, and everything else simply left his head.

"Come here. I want to drink from you as well." She moved toward him when she was as naked as he was, and he sat up on the couch to reach her. Pulling her pussy to his mouth, he licked the trickle of cream on her thigh before he buried his mouth over her heat. Vinnie screamed out what Mitch hoped to be the first of many climaxes.

She tasted of everything he could think of that was his favorite. Dark rich chocolate. Wine that had aged well, with just enough sweetness in it to have him coming back for more. Steak done just right, and strawberry cheesecake with whipped cream, the real kind, not from a tub or a can. Mitch sucked her clit and then nipped at the nubbin to hear her screaming once again. His mouth flooded with her juices.

"No more." She pulled back from him, and he growled low. "Please. I need to feel you inside of me. I want to come while you fuck me."

Leaning back against the couch, he helped her settle over him. He held his aching cock as gently as he could as she lowered her heat onto him. When he was buried to the root, her body fitting tightly over his, he held her hips while she rolled them back and forth, her hands holding onto his shoulders as her head was thrown back in pleasure.

"Christ, do you have any idea how lovely you are right now?" She moaned an answer, and he leaned forward and took her breast into his mouth. The tip was hard, the breast soft and firm. When he bit down on her nipple again, he felt her tighten around him and did it again and again until she started riding him harder, faster. "Come for me, Vinnie. I want to see your face when you come on me like this."

Her body bowed back, and her hair, normally up in some sort of knot, came tumbling down and touched his balls. He nearly came just from that, the soft curling of her hair setting off all kinds of feelings in his body he'd ever felt before. And when she came this time, her nipples grew even tighter. Her fingers dug deeply into his shoulders hard enough that he could feel blood, and he saw a kind of beauty in her he knew he'd never see again. Victoria Graham was, simply put, the most beautiful creature in the universe.

He rolled her to her back when she looked at him, the couch just big enough that he could fuck her this way but little else. They took it to the floor, her legs wrapping around his hips as he went deeper within her, his cock stretching to fill every part of her. His balls ached with the desire to empty into her, his cock yearning to fill her.

"You have to drink from me." He looked at the pounding pulse at her throat and felt a craving he'd never experienced before. Need for her, to taste her like this, was making him hungry to have her all. "I'm going to cut my vein, and I want to you drink from me when we come. I'm going to bite you as well. Please do this for me...for us. I want you to bond with me in ways you can't imagine."

Mitch wanted her, her blood and body, as he fucked her liked he'd never fucked before. Everything about her was his, and he wanted to...no, he *needed* to lay claim to her. As soon as her nails scraped across her throat and blood began to seep from the wound, he came, his entire body turned on by the thought of sucking her into him. Mitch sucked the wound hard even as his cock continued to empty inside of her. The first taste of her made him come again, his world rocking off its foundations over and over again.

The heat of her mouth at his own throat had him wanting more even as her teeth bit into him, tearing his flesh. He came again, screaming around the wound at her throat even as she tightened once again, her body coming with his as she drank deeply.

Mitch saw stars first, then darkness. Just before he knew he was going to pass out, he felt...energized. His heart began to beat harder, his mind, rarely quiet, felt full. Images that were not his own began to fill in the places he never knew he'd had. Her memories became his, and he knew they were one. Licking at the wound, he wondered how he'd seal it when he looked down and saw that it was no longer there. Mitch was spent and couldn't have moved if he had to.

Her arms fell away from him, and he tried really hard not to simply drop on top of her like dead weight. As he rolled, pushing over the table beside them, Mitch was very proud of the fact that not only had he been able not to hurt her, but he had her atop him now. Her body felt like the best blanket he'd ever touched over him. And when she sat up, his cock still deep inside of her, he watched her face as she gave him a slow, comfortable ride.

"Mitch, I love you." He felt his heart tighten in his chest, and he wasn't sure what to tell her. "I know your life, all of it, just as you do mine. But I want you to know that no matter what happened to you, it will never have anything to do with us."

He lay there, his heart beating again and his mind slowed so he could think. "He raped me nightly, and when he didn't, she did. And when they were finished with me, they'd take me out into the yard and hose me off like I was nothing more than an animal."

"They should be killed, not rewarded for what they did to you. And the others." He started to look away, but she said his name. "You have to tell them. The police, your lawyer, as well as the others. The Bruces need to pay for what they did."

Mitch moved then. He didn't want her touching him. He felt...dirty. His skin crawled along his body, and he itched with the need to be clean. When she held him to her, leaning over him so he couldn't escape, he had to let out long breaths or scream in horror at the images that were running in a long loop in his head.

Night after night, he'd been tied to the bed with cuffs, his body beaten when he didn't cooperate. His food had been taken away when he didn't satisfy either of them. Mitch hadn't been the only one, either. All the boys there had been treated the same way, humiliated and beaten, when all they ever wanted was to have somewhere safe to be.

"Just breathe, baby. I have you." Vinnie might have said that more than once, but he'd been so terrified, the little boy again, that he'd not heard her. His mind felt close to shutting down, and he knew she was right. He had to talk about it to someone. As she continued to hold him, Mitch began his tale. It was the first time in all his life he felt as if he could talk about the things that had been done to him and the others.

"My parents had been gone for about a year when I was sent to them. They were killed in an accident when I was about fourteen years old. I was in the system for about a year before I went to live with the Bruces." He took a long slow breath as he continued, "Carol Bruce, she would come into my room or in the shower where I was and blow me. At first it was just her, and at fifteen it wasn't that bad. I mean...I never turned her down, but I did feel like I'd been hurt somehow by her. Dirty. That's what it felt like when she'd leave me, I was dirty. Then one night...that night things changed forever for me." Closing his eyes, he tried not to feel but only to speak. "Mark came into the shower with Carol and watched us. He was naked by the time I came down her throat, and his cock was hard and wet. I was sickened by it. But he jerked off all over the two of us and had Carol lick it off me. He laughed at me then when I tried to tell them that I was done with it. I didn't want to...I know that as a young man I should have wanted sex all the time, but not like this, not with them."

"What did he do then?" Mitch got up then as she'd moved to the couch. He pulled on his pants as she took his shirt over her head and watched him. "Mitch, I need for you to tell me everything. I can see it, feel what they did to you, but I want you to tell me."

"You'll hate me." She told him that was never going to be possible. "But I let them...I allowed them to take me as they wanted for another year after that."

"You didn't allow them to do anything to you, Mitch. They tied you up. They forced you." He paced, thinking about the night before he'd run. "Mitch?"

"There were chains on all the beds. From the very beginning I had noticed them. And I never really gave it any thought when they'd come in and chain one of the other boys to the bed at night. But I never heard anything, so I never...I think they drugged us so they could do those things to us. I never...it wasn't anything that happened to me, so if anything was brought up, I never heard it. I know now that they more than likely gave us something with our evening meal, and only tied up the ones that they were going to use who had not been drugged." He walked to the window and looked out into the darkened yard. There were things moving about, things he was sure were there to protect them, but didn't ask. It wasn't important right now. "The night before I left, they had chained me and this other boy to our beds. I was screaming to be let go, telling them that I wanted to run. I guess in hindsight, that was the wrong thing to say to them, but they came in naked, both of them, and stood over our beds. It wasn't the first time, of course, that I'd seen them do this to me, but it was the first time they'd had two of us. We were the only two boys there, I think." His mind wandered to that night and the horrors of it. Mitch felt himself slide into the dream that had haunted him every night since he was a kid.

"What are you going to do to us?" Mitch remembered the other boy, Thomas was his name, screaming at them to back the fuck off when they got close to the bed. Mitch told them again he wanted no part of this. "You leave us alone. We don't want you to touch us."

Thomas kicked out at Carol when she came at him, grabbing him by the leg to flip him over onto his back. Thomas hit her once, knocking her back far enough that she hit her head and blacked out. Mitch was working at the cuff at his arm when he felt someone touch his naked flesh at his shoulder.

Looking up at the dick right in front of his face, he knew that Mark was going to make him take him into his mouth, something he'd done before while Carol had held him tight in her arms. He'd tried his best to bite the man, but she'd held his mouth open and he had to take him. It had sickened him for a week after. That was when he saw the ghost right behind Mark.

"A calmness seemed to settle over me, like I knew that this would be the last time anyone touched me this way again. The boy, I have no idea what his name was, simply put his hand out and touched the cuff at my wrist. It was then that I noticed the ones on my legs were already off. The lock opening made me reach up to grab Mark by the dick and twist." Mitch thought about that day a lot, even when he didn't want to. "He screamed, his body falling backward against the wall as I watched the ghost touch the cuffs on Thomas's legs and arms. I ran after that. Stayed on the streets until I was old enough to find a job for myself and stop stealing. I've...it's been a goal of mine to pay back the people that I took from. I'm working through that all the time."

"You called the state on the Bruces. But you never told them what they'd done to you." Mitch shook his head. "Why not? Don't you think it would have made it easier on the others had you done that?"

"No. They'd been taken care of so that they'd not be having sex with any of their charges again. That I know." She asked him how. "The other children...they had killed two of the others that had been there and buried them in the back. I've gone to talk to them a couple of times or they came to find me. They protect, I guess you could say. Haunt them so they're not able to go into the bedrooms to harm again."

"Good. That's wonderful. I never knew that ghosts could...I guess I should have guessed you'd not leave the others to be hurt." He turned and looked at her, and when she smiled, he smiled with her. "Are you hungry? I'm not, but I could watch you eat. I've had Hugo bring in some food for you. If there is anything you don't like or that you want, just—"

"Did you hear what I said? I said that they're being haunted, and I made that happen." She stood up, and he was disappointed when she wrapped a blanket from the back of the couch around her waist so that it covered her long lean legs. "I used what I can do to make their lives hell."

"And I think that's great. You have kept others safe with what you can do. You didn't abuse what you were born with. Don't assume, Mitch. You know that only makes an ass of you and me. I love that you did that. You more than likely saved countless other children by doing it." She smiled, and he could see her fangs. "We're just going to have to make them pay more."

Mitch followed her into the kitchen and wondered for the first time in his life how the hell he'd gotten so lucky. First, there were Steele and Ray and the other men, and now her. Mitch thought in that moment he might just be able to win against the Bruces after all.

Chapter 5

Darling, I can't enter your house. What's going on? She'd been trying to contact Vinnie for the past ten minutes through their connection, and it just wasn't working. Amber looked around when her daughter didn't answer her. Something was keeping her not just from the house, but the land as well. Every time she started to step over the boundaries of some...well, hidden line, she felt herself burn, like she'd been staked out in the sun. She looked at her mate, dead now, when he growled at her.

"Well? Why aren't you going in? I'm telling you right now, I've never seen a more labyrinth house in my life. Those underground tunnels are driving me crazy just trying to keep which way I've been or where I need to go again. I need to get to her lair." She reached for her daughter again, telling her to come let her in as Horatio continued. "When I get in there where she rests, you'll come to me then and we'll take care of her."

"There is something wrong here. I can't cross over into her domain, nor can I get her to talk to me. It more than likely has to do with that fucking Mitch, I'm thinking. He's put some sort of spell on the house that is blocking me as well. I told her she needed to get rid of him, and now he's got her doing things against me that just isn't right." She wanted to snarl at them all, but knew better than to do so with Horrie. "Mother told me all about the house and how Luther showed up to show her what he'd done. She even told me how she'd had help looking up her own builder to see if he had something hidden. She was telling me that that bastard Luther showed her the doorway we've been using...or I've been using. Fucking bastard. Someone needs to tear his eyes out. What the hell was he doing hanging about anyway?"

"More than likely hoping to see her in the nude. That boy, the one that has been around, do you know if they're really mates or not? You know, sometimes it's just a simple lust thing. Like I had with that woman a long time ago." She said that they were. "Damn it all to hell and back. You know that will mess things up for us. We need to get into the house and make it ours. And soon."

Amber nodded. She missed her mate, more and more all the time. And the fact that her daughter had...well, murdered her own father had made her both sad and angry at the same time. He was a good man on occasion, and when he was good, he was very good. Every person had bad days. His were just...well, his were more violent, yes, but they were a violent-natured species. She'd thought that Vinnie would just tie him up for a bit, let him burn a little, then let him go. It shouldn't have mattered that the council had ordered her to end his life. It was her father, and she shouldn't have been able to harm him. Then they'd told her she had to watch him die. It had been too much for her, and she'd gone into her crypt to hide away her pain. Amber had mourned him for months before he'd finally come to her and told her of his plan.

They were going to take her house. Seemed innocent enough, she supposed, but the house, with all of its tunnels, would take them places not even their magic would. And they could hide away, deep in them if the house were to catch fire or be raided. The house had been built by a vampire for a vampire to live in. Vinnie only used part of the expansive house, and she and her Horrie wanted it all. And the things he'd found in it when he'd been looking around. Money for one thing…more than either of them ever had.

"Has she answered you yet?" Amber told him she had not. "How is she blocking you, I ask? It is bad enough she was able to kill her own sire, but to block her mother? Unheard of. Try again and keep trying until the little cunt answers you. She's going to have a lot to answer to when I get to her."

Amber wanted to point out that it obviously wasn't unheard of, but she didn't say anything. Even dead, Horrie had more power than she did, and to have him mad at her again would be painful. Plus, when he was upset, he tended to interrupt her rest, and she needed that when dealing with her daughter. A tired vampire was a stupid one. Making mistakes would cost her her life if she wasn't rested and careful all the time.

Vinnie had always been a very independent child. Most of the time, Horrie and she would go away for long periods, only to return and find her just as they'd left her, tending the house and gardens, keeping the bills paid up when there was money to do so, getting herself fed and clothed, and going to classes. It wasn't until she turned twenty-five, the age of maturity, that either of them took any notice of her. Her power base was greater than either of theirs. And Amber's mother, Vinnie's grandmother...well, she was more a part of her life than Amber had ever been. Which, most of the time, suited Amber just fine. Until now.

"Do you suppose she knows about what we have planned?" Horrie told her not to be ridiculous. The child was stupid. "I don't know about that, Horrie. She did figure out about what you were doing all the time. She knew before the council had come to her to end your life. Then there was Millie."

"That was and always will be her fault. Had Millie just listened to what I said, then she'd be here with you instead of wandering around lost. She is by far one of...why do you think this child of yours is ignoring you?" Vinnie was always her child when she wasn't doing what Horrie wanted her to. "Call to her again. Tell her that you demand that she come let you in."

Millie had never liked her. In fact, Amber was sure that had she had her way, she would have been staked to the ground with Millie's brother and not walking around like she still was. Amber had seen Millie a couple of times since she'd been killed. A madman had taken it into his head to kill all vampires, and it just so happened he started and finished with Millie. He'd staked her through her heart, but she'd been able to tear his throat out in the process, ending his plans with a swipe of her sharp claws.

When Amber saw the car pulling into the drive she was near, she moved deeper into the woods surrounding the property. Horrie just stood there as if he had no reason to hide when she remembered that he didn't. The dead, as he was, were invisible to humans. The moving van coming in right behind the large SUV had her worried and made

Horrie curse up a storm. This would not bode well for either of them.

"She's moving him in. Damn it, I didn't give her permission to let him into our house. Did you? Do you have any idea what that will do to our plans? A necromancer. A fucking necromancer in our house." Amber said nothing and watched the house. "I'm telling you right now, Amber love, I am not happy with this. You will tell her that you aren't either. Move him out or kill him, I don't care which, but I do not want him living in my home while I'm there. If he does, all will be lost."

There were several things she wanted to ask her mate, most of which centered on why they hadn't bought the house in the first place. Luther had offered it to them. Said that the house was special. Then a week after they said they'd think on it, they found out that he'd out and sold it to Vinnie. And the child would not allow them to move in with her. She had told them that this was her own home, and she wanted to make it such. That had been more decades ago than she could remember. And she was still not allowing her, her own mother, to move in even now.

Of course, there wasn't any way for them to have been able to afford the house. Neither of them had saved a single penny since they'd turned into great vampires. When they had money, it filtered through their hands like water. Here now and gone in seconds. Vinnie had it, lots of it. Amber's mother did as well. And both of them were being selfish with it. Her mother had never been very good about giving her any, but Vinnie had told her she was finished too. What a horrid thing to say to your own mother. To tell her that she was on her own from now on. Whatever was she supposed to do now?

Then there were the reasons Horrie wanted the house. To keep them safe. He was dead, pretty much as safe as he could get so far as she knew. No one could kill him. He could be out during the day, and there was nothing stopping him from moving in the house anyway. Up until today, that was. She, however, was still trying to get to a room where she could rest without being disturbed. The last few weeks she'd been at her mother's, unknown to her, of course. Her mother would tell her to stay away and to find her own home. Amber knew there had to be something more to Vinnie's house than Horrie was telling her, something she was missing.

"I don't like not having my own home anymore. I hate sleeping in a different place every night." She'd not realized she'd spoken aloud until he asked her what was wrong with doing it that way. "Most of the rooms I can find are too small. And there are no beds in any of the rooms that Mother has but on the upper levels. I can't sleep up there. Then there's only the three little places in the garage where I can go if the doors have been bolted against me. Nothing is as pretty as Vinnie says she has. Mother's house is all right in a pinch, Horrie, but I want my own place. With my own crypt and place to rest. Vinnie doesn't even have room like we did when we had a place. Did you know that you could sleep in a bed, too, should you want to? I thought that only a coffin would do. How did she find this out?"

"Your mother." Amber nodded. Now that she thought on it, her mother did sleep in a bedroom too. She had no carpet there, and there wasn't any kind of cool air blowing all the time, but she had a bed. Vinnie said that she had a room much like the ones on the upper floors, with even a bathroom and shower, as well as a closet she could store her things in. "Why are you mooning over something that you can't do a damned thing about when your daughter is being disrespectful to us?"

Amber reached out to her again, only to feel like she was butting against a hard wall. "Perhaps she is not even about." Which Amber knew was incorrect. The van and the car were being unloaded all the time, and she was sure that Vinnie was directing them. Amber wondered again what sort of things Luther had told her daughter, and what sort of things Horrie knew. She was always in the dark about things going on that she was involved in. "I should have gone over to Vinnie's house earlier as well. But I was so busy getting things out of Mother's house that I had no idea that she'd even gone there until it was too late. I wonder if she's figured out that I knew all along about the tunnels."

"Doubtful. I don't care about that right now. What I want to do is fuck you. Or watch you fucking yourself. Now." She looked at Horrie. He had that tone again, one that made her blood boil with need, and she leaned against the tree when he told her to. "Take it off, Amber. I want to see you naked again. And when you are, I'm going to watch you get that pussy of yours fucked while I watch you."

She had no idea why he wanted her to do this, but she would come so hard while he watched her. The man standing in the shadows didn't bother her. Horrie had gotten him for her, and she was happy with whatever he wanted her to do with him. The man came forward when Horrie told him to.

"I want you to eat her pussy. Eat it loudly, too. I want to hear you moaning and slurping at her." She hated that word but hurried through her undress. When she was naked, the man, a young man of about thirty, dropped to his knees in front of her and pulled her pussy to his mouth.

Amber loved oral sex, the way the person eating her would suck at her clit and fuck her with his fingers. Every time she came, she would scream out her release just to let everyone know she was having fun. She knew that Horrie loved to hear her enjoyment, and she never held back when she didn't have to.

The man eating her sucked on her clit more and more as she came. And she did, several times as he ate her. She played with her breasts and nipples, and she looked at Horrie when she told him she was coming, her pussy on fire for the feel of a thick cock. When the man pulled back, her body was needy. That sort of sex was good, but she needed more, much more.

"Fuck her." She felt her pussy gush with new liquid as the man stood up. His clothing came off in shreds as the two of them tore at it. When he was as naked as her, she wrapped her hand around his thick cock and fisted him while he rocked into her hand. To have him come on her this way was something she knew she'd enjoy, but it would disappoint Horrie. He liked to watch, and she had to give him what he wanted. "Fuck her. Take her hard and from behind."

Amber got to the ground with her ass in the air. The moment that man sank his cock into her, she knew Horrie had taken his body. He didn't care if she would come so long as he was enjoying himself with a pussy. As she was nearly taken to the ground, she felt fingers touch her clit, then pull hard enough on it that she cried out in pain. But Horrie never stopped as he continued to fuck her well after the human had come.

This kind of sex she didn't care for. It was all right, she supposed, for the man. But for her, it was a disappointment. She was flipped over as soon as the cock in her pussy was gone, and she nearly screamed when the man went back to her pussy and began eating her. Not for pleasure, she didn't think, but almost as if he were really going to eat her. Amber came five times as Horrie and the man nearly tore her in two with the human's mouth and hands. And he fucked her again, blood seeping from her body. She then tore at the man's throat when Horrie told her to feed.

Drinking deeply of the man, his blood still hot as she drank from him, she watched her mate as he stood over them, his cock limp in his cold hands. She knew that as soon as she was finished, the man would just be left where he was, his body to be found or not by anyone walking by. She almost felt sorry for him, but continued to roll her hips up to get more and more relief while she drank from the man who had given her pleasure. When she was done, had her fill, instead of sealing the wounds that would keep him from bleeding out, she tossed him off her and rubbed the fresh blood from his throat over her body.

Fingering her pussy, she came twice more, the blood making the slide of her fingers much easier than when she would do it alone. And when Horrie roared at her, telling her to stop, she brought herself once more, then disappeared. If she stayed when he was in that state, he'd hurt her again, and Amber needed to be healthy to take on her mother and daughter. There was no doubt that she was going to have to do just that if she was ever going to get into her daughter's home again.

~~~

Vinnie wasn't sure what to do now. Mitch was moving through her house, not like he owned it, but more like he was a guest. And that wasn't the way she wanted this relationship to start out. He was asking her if he could use the office, the books, and the television. Which, if she was honest with herself, she hadn't even known they had until then. She wanted him to be at home, not wondering if he could touch things.

"Hum, Vinnie?" She looked at him and could see on his face that something was wrong. "You should know that I can see your father out there, and a woman. I'm not sure it's your mother or not, but.... Also your aunt. She's not with them, but is there all the same."

"Where?" She got up to go to the window where he was and couldn't see anything more than the trees and drive. "I can't see her. Are you sure that it's them?"

"Yes. And he's naked. Your aunt is...oh."

"What?"

"Your mother just left, sort of just disappeared. She's gone now, but she was there with him, also naked. Your aunt is there, but I don't think they see her. Or perhaps they do and don't care."

She was glad now that she could not see them. "They can have sex when they're dead?" He told her no, her father was just watching her. "Oh. Oh, I get it. She's performing for him. Not that that makes it any better, but I'm glad to know they're not having sex on my front lawn. Mother has been trying to get me to answer her, did you know that? I think she's found out she can no longer come here."

"Just those you invite, Steele said. And that might be tricky, too, since if they come here with the intent to cause harm, it won't let them enter." Vinnie nodded. "Have you contacted your grandmother yet? She'll also need to be invited. If you want her to come here, that is."

"I do and yes, I'm going to talk to her the next time I see her. She said she'd be by sometime this evening." Yawning again, she moved back from the window as the sun started to make its way across the floor toward her. "I have to go to rest soon. And...I don't want to leave you, but I have to rest. I've not been doing that well lately, and it's starting to catch up with me."

"I understand." He moved, and she could see the mark at his throat. When he caught her staring, he put his fingers over the bite mark and smiled at her. "Will anyone else see it? Not that I care, but I would like to know."

"No. Just other vampires. Maybe your friends. I don't know that much about necros other than they...well, they used to scare the crap out of me. You'd not believe the kind of stories I heard growing up. And grandmother has a few of her own too." She did know a little more than she had. First of all, while they could call up the dead, she'd been told that only a few of them could actually do it. Steele could, as well as Addie. However, Addie was still learning things.

Ray was strong as well. But he was really nice and kept them all in line and safe. Raising the dead, as in a vampire, was only something that Steele could do for now.

Nick was talented too, stronger than the rest save Steele and his wife, but he was gaining more and more daily. Landon was...he was harder to read than the rest. "Laid back" didn't really describe him so much as it was him. Drew was nice, but he was a loner. Hard working, but didn't hang out as much as the rest did in any kind of group setting. Hugh had a chip on his shoulder was the only way she thought to describe him. Not against them or even her, but people in suits. He simply hated them all. Vinnie wondered if there was something there that no one knew about.

As she made her way to the lower levels with Mitch at her side, she thought about all the turns and twists she'd found when they'd gone exploring the house last night. The doorway that had been in her study had not been the only doorway, of course, but it had been the biggest find so far. She paused outside her rooms when they reached them.

"There is a direct route to here. You think that's what they were looking for?" Mitch asked her what they could do to her once they made it this far. "Nothing if they can't get in, but my father could, couldn't he?"

"Yes. But I don't think he can do much more than...can you open the door from the inside? Or is there a combination nearby that he can give to someone on this side?" She told him no, it was opened on either side by fingerprints, hers. "I see. Then there might be a way for him to make it work. This is...I'm only guessing here, but he could take your body for a minute or two once he was in your room. It would drain him, but he could do it, then take you to the door and open it by placing your hand over the reader. Like I said, it would drain him, but he'd be in here with you. And if your mom is in on this, and I have no doubt that she is, then she could enter, kill you, and that would be the end of it. Why though?"

"I have no idea." And she didn't either. Going into the bedroom suite, she showed him around. There was as much floor space on this level as there was on the one above her. And she used very little of it, she just realized. But having Mitch there with her made her think that they might from now on.

There was a bedroom, as well as a huge bathroom with a shower and tub. There were several walk-in closets, but only a few of them had any actual clothing in them. A living room with a computer was set up in one corner, as well as a landline phone that she could use if the service to the house was blocked. She did have cell service down here, but if the power was off for any length of time that would be useless as well.

There were no windows to let the sunshine in, only one more exit that didn't use the door she showed him now, a large storage of old books, and the vault she'd had put in when she bought the house. In it was cash, a great deal of it, her jewelry she'd collected over the years, and the things her grandmother had given her.

"I'm going to show you how to get in, then I'm going to put your prints on this reader. Once you put your hand on it, you're going to feel a small pinch. It's taking a sample of your blood. It'll do that every time you use it. It's a secondary safety that I've had put in."

He nodded. "Good idea." As he put his hand over the reader for her after she'd set it up for him to be added, he smiled at her. "I won't come in unless you say it's okay. I mean, I know how much you'll need your —"

"I want you to come in any time you want. I want you to treat this house as your own. All the time. Because it is your home now. As much as it is mine." He nodded, but she could tell he wasn't going to. "I want you to be a part of my life, and that includes this house and the things we now own together. Like the cars and the other things. There is...Mitch, you're my mate, which means that we're together forever."

"Until I die." She shook her head. This was something that she'd spoken to her grandmother about as well. "What do you mean, no? I'm just...well, basically a human."

"No, you're only half right on that. You're human, yes, but you're not going to die. Not so long as I live. Hugo either. When I took you into my heart you became a part of me. My blood will give you the ability to heal much faster; you're going to be able to move quicker too. Not like I can, but fast. Your body will be able to take more as well. A bullet to the body, so long as it's not to the heart, will not kill you. A shot to the head will kill you, if it's in the right place. Otherwise, you are like this superhuman. Broken bones will only take hours to heal rather than weeks, and you'll never get sick again, not from the flu or even any kind of diseases, including cancer."

He didn't move when she took his hand off the reader, but she knew he was thinking. Vinnie wasn't sure if he was upset or not…he had the most unreadable face she'd ever seen. But the longer he stood there, the more nervous she got, until he pulled her to him and kissed her like he meant it. Breathless when he lifted his head, all she could do was smile at him before she trusted herself to speak again.

"What was that for?" Instead of answering her, he kissed her again, taking his time as he tasted her, her body craving what he was giving her. "Mitch, I have to rest, but if you keep that up, you're not leaving here."

"I wanted to tell you that…while I'm not sure if I love you yet, I do care for you a great deal. And this gift that you've given me, I will not abuse it." He kissed her again, and using the reader, left the room, closing the door softly behind him. She stood there, frustrated and happy at the same time. She was going to make him pay for this.

Going to her bed, she stripped down and lay on the covers. She had a mate. She also had a father who was coming for her, a mother that was in on it, and an aunt that hated her almost as much as she did her. But for so many reasons, Vinnie didn't care about all that. She had a mate. And that was all she could focus on.

"Child, I must have a word with you." Vinnie sat up on the bed when her grandmother appeared. She wasn't really there, but her image was just as clear as if she was. "Your mother is in with Horatio. And Millicent is there as well, but I'm not finding her in on any of the things that they're about."

"How did you find out?" As far as Vinnie was concerned, if her grandmother said it, it was a fact. "And what are their plans?"

"I don't know what they think they're going to do, but they want this house and all that's in it. Not you, of course. That would just be too good. No, this house. What does it have that you can think of?" She told her of the tunnels behind the wall that Luther had shown them. "I would...that would be a way to get around the city if they opened up there. Do you suppose they can? And once they have it...what do you suppose they want this house for at this time?"

"I have no idea. Really, I don't. We looked, but there are so many tunnels that we had to back track a great deal." She suggested that she send down Hugo. "That's a wonderful idea. He could do it. Sniff his way around better than we could. I'll send him now."

"Good. And while you're at it, have that young man of yours move in with you." She told her that he'd moved in today. "You're wonderfully smart, my dear. How did your parents never see that before?"

"They're too wrapped up in whatever Father was doing to care, I guess." Her grandmother agreed with her. "But this is my house and I'm not giving it up without a fight. But what I don't understand is, when Luther put it up for sale, they were offered it first. And when they told him that they weren't interested, I got it. Is it because I own it that it bothers them so much?"

"I think, and as much as it pains me to say this, I think they want it because they're selfish people who would take candy from a baby should they want it. Hell, my dear, even if they didn't want it, they'd take it." Her grandmother looked around, then back at her. "Mason said to tell you that he's got a few of his buddies looking out for your man as well. I think that's a wonderful idea. I've also sent him to watch over the others of the household as well. There is no reason for them to be hurt in the crossfire, so to speak."

"Thank you. But I'd let Steele know if I were you. He's a nice enough man, but I'd not like to have him as an enemy. He seems...you know that controlled sort of anger that you say I have?" Her grandmother said that she did. "I think Steele is better at it. He has this angry calmness about him that scares me and impresses me. But I'd tell him." She said she would first thing.

After they discussed a few more things, her grandmother started to leave. But Vinnie called her back for one more thing. It was something that she'd been thinking about for some time. And after talking it over with Mitch, he thought it was a good idea as well. The house needed more people in it, he told her.

"Come live with us." Her grandmother looked so shocked that she stared open mouthed at her as Vinnie continued. "We would love to have you here. And this place is certainly big enough for us to live here and never see each other. There are four other apartments down here with mine you'd be able to stay in. And that way you can get to know Mitch a little better."

"I'll have to think on it." She didn't say no, and that thrilled Vinnie to no end. "What of my house here? Whatever would I do with it?"

"Sell it. Rent it out. I don't care. You know as well as I do we both have enough money we'd never have to worry about it even if it should sit there and rot. But I'd like you

here all the time, not popping in and out. I love you."
Grandmother told her she loved her as well. "Then you
really will think about it?"

"Yes. But I think we should get his other business taken
care of first. Your parents aren't just going to go away, and
we both know that." Vinnie told her she agreed. "Then
when the dust settles, we'll talk more about this, all right?"

"Yes. But they won't be changing my mind. I want you
here and so does Mitch. He's as excited about it as I am."
Her grandmother blew her a kiss and left her. Vinnie laid
down and fell into a deep sleep almost immediately.

Chapter 6

Connie watched Mitch. He was certainly happier, but he was also quieter than usual. She wondered about the envelope in his hand and started several times to ask him about it, but she wasn't sure it was any of her business. But when Aster moved over his shoulder and read it, Connie wanted to kiss the child.

"They're very serious about this, aren't they?" Mitch told Aster to stop being a brat. "I'm not a brat. I'm as old as you are...well, about anyway. But those people, the Bruces, what do they think they can get from you if they come around here?"

"Anything they want, I suppose. But I'm not going to sit by and let them. Vinnie hooked me up with a good attorney, and he's looking into some things." Mitch looked away from them both, and Connie wondered if he'd told the attorney what had happened to him in that house. "I talked to Vinnie about it as well. I told her what I had to go through when I lived there. Everything."

"Good." He turned to look at her when she spoke. "You need to have people know what they did to you. I know it hurts, but you did nothing wrong, and they're the ones that need to be punished." He nodded but said nothing. "Are you thinking people will think less of you because of what happened? If they do, you let me know, and I'll show them a thing or two that a ghost can do."

"I'm not really worried about that any more. I was, but not now. But I'm just wondering, who do you think they'll believe? A broken down man with not a pot to piss in, or people that have been watching the unwanted for most of their lives? I'm pretty sure I don't even come close to the image that they project for the world to see. The Bruces, I mean. I've seen some of the things they've said about me, and none of it is very nice." Mitch snorted. "I have little to nothing to show for my life. Some money in the bank. A steady job and some friends that are less than human. A soon-to-be wife that is a good attorney too, but she's a little on the odd side in that she's a vampire. I love that about her, but I'm pretty sure it won't win me any prizes in the upstanding citizen awards. Oh, and let's not forget that I have long, very helpful conversations with two of the sweetest ghosts I know."

"Thank you, darling. We love talking to you as well. But you're thinking too hard about this. Why, I know for a fact those people have been under investigation several times since you left them. There are three boys missing. Did you know that?" He told her he did and was looking for them as well. "Mitch, you can't just let this go. Please tell me you're going to fight them with everything you have."

"I had thought to just figure out a way to pay them off. Or at the very least, run away and start over with the help of a new name and identity. But since I've found someone to love and to love me back, I think I'm going to hit them with all I have, thanks to you and the others." He sat up and leaned back more on the fence that surrounded the little family cemetery. "On a different note, I've moved in with Vinnie. I asked her and she said it was on her mind to tell me to anyway. But Christ, you should see this house. It has nine bedrooms on the second floor and five more on the third. They all have their own bathrooms too. And the lower levels are like this entire new house that no one sees but her and me."

"I've talked to Luther about the house. He's very proud of that mansion. You'll be happy there." He nodded but didn't look all that convinced. "Tell me what's bothering you, Mitch. I can help some. Maybe."

"They've named Vinnie in the suit. Not with me, but as part of it. Because she is in my life and has money, I guess. I don't understand some people." Connie didn't either, and she'd seen more than her fair share of them. "Now they want even more. And they think that the state should continue to pay them as if they're watching children for them for the rest of their lives. At some point, you'd think they'd have a clue that what they were doing was wrong. I understand that they've been investigated, but it seems no one looked all that hard to find anything. Why are there people like them out there?"

"I don't know, love. I truly don't. People like them are always looking for the short cut. It might not be millions of dollars, though most of them would jump at it, but mostly to make it so that they can get as much as they can from the system because they feel they deserve it. Even if they don't, they'll keep taking and taking, complaining about how they can never get ahead this way." Connie looked at her home, the one her lovely family lived in. "Mitch, if you don't fight this with every fiber of your being, I'm going to be very disappointed in you."

"I've decided to fight. I don't want to, but they've pushed me against the wall, and it's either go at them with all I have or let them continue to beat me down. And they are. Daily now. There was an interview on television last night with them. You should have heard the drivel they were saying. How I did them wrong by telling the state I was no longer there, when in fact I was there the entire time. They claimed I even talked others into saying untrue things as well. Accused them of doing things that just weren't right. I never told anyone why I left until now, but they have this version of it in their heads that is making me look like a pervert." Connie asked him what they were. "They said that Mark told me that I couldn't make passes at his wife, that I needed to have counseling. To see someone about what was going on in my head. Basically, he said I was nuts. They said that they were going to call the board on me anyway, but the way I'd done it hurt them. It was the way they'd ran things all along and no one had complained until I told them to. Bullshit."

She smiled. This was a Mitch she'd not seen before. Fired up and full of piss and vinegar, as she used to say. Connie wondered if she could do anything to help her friend when she realized that some of those boys he'd told her about were dead. In all these years of being gone, Connie had made some very strong connections and was going to reach out to one of them as soon as Mitch left. There was no sense in stirring the pot up if it didn't lead anywhere, so she'd wait to tell him. When Mitch stood up to leave, she wanted to hug him to her desperately. She so loved this young man.

"Well, Steele is saying we need to go over a few things in the office. I think he wants to make sure that none of what we do is brought up at the trial. I've even asked him not to go, and he only laughed at me." Mitch smiled and so did Connie. "I've never seen such a change in a person as he made when he met Kari. Do you suppose everyone does to a degree?"

"You have." Connie nodded when Aster spoke. "You're not as dark or moody. I've even seen you smile a couple of times for no reason whatsoever. My goodness, it's like someone took your body and replaced it with a happy one. I like this new you. But what I'd like to know is, when are you going to introduce us to your mate? And when are you going to invite us to your home so we can come and see you whenever we want?"

"She can't see you." Aster asked him why not. "I'm not sure. I've asked her a couple of times if she can see her aunt or dad when he's around, but she can't. I've been meaning to ask Steele about it."

"She doesn't want to see us." Mitch asked her what she meant. Connie knew there were many factors involved in seeing a ghost, but if you believed you could, then you could. "She's afraid of you being a necromancer, isn't she? That's what it is. She's in love with you and is still slightly afraid. I know she and Steele have talked, even Kari and Addie have, but she's still afraid of what you might be able to do to her. Not that she really believes it in her heart, but her mind is harder to convince sometimes."

"I'd never hurt her. She has to know that of me." Connie told him of course he wouldn't. "So you think that if she only believes in me and what I can do, she can see what I do? All of you guys?"

"I don't know. I really don't. The fact that you can see us at all is a wonderment to me. Did you know there are more of you guys than I first thought? I mean, like families of you." He said he'd figured that was true. "But did you know most of them are taking drugs, living in homes for the mentally unstable as well? People think they're insane and they usually end their own lives rather than have anyone there to help them. That is the saddest thing I've ever heard, don't you think?"

"Yes I do. And had it not been for Ray and him finding me, I might have been there as well. But how? How do you help them? I'm sure you have a plan. You'd have never brought it up if you didn't." She laughed and so did he. "I tell you what. You let me finish this thing up with the Bruces and I'll help you with your plans. I don't have much in the way of funding, but it's all yours if we can make this work."

As he moved back to the house, his step a little lighter, Aster came to stand beside her. The girl had had her life cut so short, but she'd been doing so much good since she'd been killed at seventeen. And Connie was sure that had she not been there with her all these years, she might have been a little worse off than even Mitch had been.

"Does he have any idea how much he's worth, you think?" Connie asked her how much. "Billions. Not just money either, but houses, cars, stocks. Vinnie has done well for herself, and in living a long time, she's also amassed a great many collectables. I think...what do you think of her opening a nice antique store? I think with her knowledge and our connections, she can make a go at it. If nothing else, she might have firsthand knowledge of all the pieces that come her way. She might have even owned them."

"What a thing to say. But you might be right. And you've been snooping again, haven't you?" Aster only grinned. "When she can see us, and I've no doubt she will soon, we'll have a long talk with her. She's going to have to do something other than being a lawyer. I wonder if she became one because of her being a real bloodsucker, or she just liked to rub it in people's faces."

"Knowing Vinnie, I'd say she did it to rub in their faces. She's a nice person. Too bad about her family." Connie agreed. She'd been using some of her more...well, less than stellar connections to keep an eye on Horatio, as well as the rest of the family. He was up to no good, she just knew it. The man was simply bad news. Connie looked at Aster when she laughed.

"Well, I'm off. I want to go and talk to Kari's baby again. She's going to be such fun when she gets here. Just a few more months and I'll be an aunt."

As Connie was left in her solitude, she thought about the people in the house and the ones that were close by. Connie loved them all, the living and the dead, and she'd do just about anything to help them. With that in mind, she reached out to a couple of her friends and put the search out for some of the young men that had been in the Bruce household. Even the dead had connections that could help.

~~~

Millicent watched the man standing in front of her in wonder. He was mean and rude, but it was his treatment of the child with him that had her wanting to tear his throat out. Something that she'd done countless times to those that would dare piss her off. But with this newfound life, this half-life, she could only watch as he fumbled through life without knowing that he was so close to death right now. And how she'd make him pay for doing that to such an innocent child, something that had never occurred to her to be bothered about until now. She didn't bother turning when she felt her brother come up behind her.

"They're meaner now than I ever thought possible when I was alive." Horrie agreed with her and laughed. "If I could only, for a moment, do something to rid the world of one more asshole, I'd do it. Why does he have to yell at his child like that? Why does he think that screaming at her will make her understand what he wants from her any better?"

Horrie touched the man, no more, and he fell into the street in front of an oncoming car. They both watched as his body was thrown high into the sky, then tumbled back down only to be hit several more times by the other oncoming cars. She turned to him with a frown on her face when the screaming started, and thought perhaps she'd like to shove him into the street now too. Not that it would hurt him much. Millie now wished she'd done it to him when they were both alive. As if he read her mind, he shook his head.

"Not today; actually, not any day. You're not to cause me harm no matter what. Do you understand me? But today I have a job for you to do. Somehow Amber has been blocked from going into Victoria's house. I want you to see if you can get in." She asked him why her. "Because, my dear sister, you owe me."

He'd been telling her that since she'd died and found him here still moving about as if he was still living. What she owed him and why was still a mystery to her. And when she asked, and she had several times, he only blew her off and told her there were too many things for him to remember. She had an idea there had never been anything she'd done that would have her owing him, but nodded to him all the same.

"Why are you still trying to get that house? It's not like it can keep you safe, you dumbass. You're already as safe as you can get. You're dead." He only glared at her. Something else she was enjoying about being dead, her brother could no longer hurt her. He could insult her, even make her cry, but he could no longer touch her. "This is all that stupid bitch's idea, isn't it? Amber has you trying to get her the house that you said no to all those decades ago. Why? Do you think you can keep it from the creditors? I don't. Just let it go, Horrie, and move on. Please."

"We neither one wanted it back then, but I find that we want it now. And why not? It's not like Victoria needs it." Sure, Millicent thought. And she was the next beauty queen of the undead. "Now, however, after we've found out about the tunnels, we want it. Plus, and Amber doesn't know this, there is a treasure in those walls."

"What sort of treasure? And what do you think you're going to do with a treasure even if there is one?" He told her. "Spend it on what, Horrie? You do know that money and jewels aren't going to help you, don't you? You're fucking dead. Why is it that you have to be reminded of that every day? I got it the first time I was told it. I don't like it, but that's neither here nor there. We're dead. And your daughter killed you because you were too stupid to do what you were told when they told you. I'm dead because I was arrogant enough to think that living forever came without a price. I paid that when someone decided that vampires were bad news. And I blame that on you too."

"No. Victoria killed me because she begged the council to let her do it for no reason whatsoever. She covered her ass and killed me. You were killed because you were and are stupid. That man didn't even know me when he went looking for a vampire. Not my name anyway. I don't care what he said to you about me killing his wife. I might have, but why did he blame me for her being dead? I was hungry and she was there. It's the way things are. But you can see now why I have to get that house." No, she didn't, and told him that. "She has to die. And when she's dead and gone, I'll be able to live in her home, using her things while I look for the treasure. If you're nice to me, more than you have been of late, I'll let you come and help me."

Millicent wasn't even going to point out, once again, that the money was useless to them. Not only that, but the house was as well. They could live anywhere they wanted, do anything they wanted at any part of the day, and who gave a shit? They were dead. But it did hurt her that he thought her death had been her own fault. The man told her as he held her with the stake at her heart that a vampire had killed his wife, and he was going to rid the world of all of them. Millie didn't have to hear her brother's name to know he'd done it. He was forever killing women for the pure joy of it. She looked at him now and wondered for the first time in her life why she had ever looked up to him.

"Why do you think this house is blocked to your wife? And I'm assuming you as well?" Millie didn't care and thought it was pretty smart of Vinnie to have blocked them all out of her life and home. The girl would certainly be safer this way. "And why do you think I'd have any better luck than she does getting in it?"

"We neither one can get past her barrier. But I think you can get in because you're not her." Millicent barely controlled the urge to hit Horrie and to roll her eyes at him. The more time she spent with her brother on this plane, the more she realized it was a miracle he had lived as long as he had. The man was dumb. And he rarely, if ever, thought things through other than he wanted it and by God, it had better be in his hands or else. More and more of late, she was thinking her niece had been right in staking him out in the sun. Millicent wanted to get as far from him as she could. "I want you to go there right now and try. You get in and then I'll have you do some things to make it so we can get in. It's a piece of cake."

Sure it was. But she said nothing to him. It would do no good to point out that the house belonged to another. That the house was keeping his own flesh and blood safe and, more to the point, he was fucking dead and didn't need the house any more than Millie did. Her brother was a moron, plain and simple.

As she willed herself to the house her niece lived in, she thought of all the times she'd envied her. Vinnie had had her shit together even as a kid, but she'd never been one to rub it in her face. And she was pretty sure, now that she thought about it, the reason she'd hated her so much was because she'd been so kind and good hearted. But not anymore. Millie found herself wanting to get to know the woman she'd become, but knew it was too late for that as well. Millie not only envied the girl her life of the living, but what she'd done to get there. Millie, like her brother, had not saved any money, made any kinds of preparation to keep safe other than her crypt, and, unlike Vinnie, Millie had had no one love her but her brother, and even that had been iffy. Even her mother had told her never to come to her again, and she'd not. Not in centuries, and now she was also dead and gone.

Vinnie would be there, in one home or another that her parents would squat in when they'd be kicked out of a place, just doing things that no kid should have been doing.

Paying the bills, making sure the staff was all paid as well. And she even got herself up and ready for school. And back then, it wasn't as big a deal to have your kids attending school as it was now. And she had Hugo.

Hugo was a shifter, or he had been. When he showed up at the house one day, his body beaten and starved, Vinnie had taken him in and kept him safe. It was years, of course, before she became what she was today, a vampire, but he'd never left her side. Not for anything. Millicent had tried to lure him away and into her bed, but he'd never strayed from Vinnie once, keeping her safe in more ways than just from harm. The shifter had been her shoulder to cry on and someone that Vinnie could talk to when her parents were out doing whatever it was they were doing. Mostly not taking care of their child.

Millie was standing in front of the house, far enough back where she could see it but not into it, when she saw the young man she'd heard about. Steele was there as well. You couldn't be a dead person without hearing his name all over the place, but she was more interested in the man with him, the mate. Millie watched him as he moved about, his lean body bent pulling weeds or whatever from the yard.

Mitch Riley was also a force to be reckoned with. He was not nearly as strong as Steele was, but he could be lethal when he needed to be. There were times, and she was sure the rumors were true, that she would find herself wishing that he'd find Horrie and deal with him. Take him out of the picture so she and even Vinnie could be safe for the rest of their days. So Millie had been laying low, not doing things that would bring attention to herself to bring his magic to her. And now this, this thing that Horrie was demanding she do for him.

She found she didn't want to do this for Horrie. Not just see if she could get in the house, but do whatever it was he would want of her once she got in. She was sure whatever it would be, it would not get her in the good graces of Vinnie's new mate or the necromancer's that could destroy her very quiet death. Standing there, she tried to think how she could get out of it short of leaving this realm.

"Can you get in?" She nearly screamed when Horrie spoke behind her. "Did you even try or are you just standing here looking at the trees? Sometimes I wonder how we were ever related. You are the dumbest person I've ever had the misfortune to be blood to."

"As do I. Every single day, Horrie." He, of course, took that as a compliment. "I haven't tried, as I've only just gotten here. And with the fact that Steele is there, I've thought to wait until I can try without getting my ass zapped. You do know who that man is, don't you? And the things he can do to one of us if he wanted to?"

"Yeah, I know who he is and what he thinks he can do to the dead. Fucker. He needs to learn his place." Millicent started to point out it was his place to take care of the humans, but she only nodded. Sometimes it was just too much to deal with Horrie, especially when he was like this. Why had she never noticed that before? "Get your ass to trying. You think we can wait around on you all fucking day?"

She reached out to see if she could get in. And when she tried again, she got the same results. She was blocked as well. Millicent was giddy with the knowledge and turned to her brother to tell him so when she saw her niece. Christ, who would have ever thought she could come from her parents and look the way she did? Not her, certainly.

"Having a mate has changed her into a real beauty." She heard her brother snarl something, but she didn't care at the moment. Vinnie was walking through the woods with a large panther. And when they both stopped, Millicent knew that one or both of them could see them. "Horrie, your daughter can see us. And I don't think she's none too happy to find us here."

"Good, then she can hear me too." He moved toward them and the panther's hair stood on end. Millicent wondered if she could do much harm to Horrie, and found that while she loved him, she didn't care if he was gone. As he approached them Millicent hung back, wanting no part of this or whatever outcome there might be from this. But she didn't leave, wanting to hear what Vinnie had to say to the man that wanted her dead too.

"Father. What is it you're doing here? I thought for sure I'd sent you to hell." He lunged at her, only to have her laugh. "That will do you no good, I'm afraid. I'm a good deal stronger than you are at the moment. Not to mention, I'd not fuck with me today. I'm not in the mood for your bullshit. Not that I ever was."

"You think so, cunt? I got news for you, you're going to pay for killing me. See if you don't, and when I'm done with you, nobody is going to want a thing to do with you." The panther growled low but didn't move. It was then that Millie realized the cat could see them as well. "What the fuck are you doing hanging around these animals anyway? You should be with your own kind."

"Like you?" He nodded at Vinnie, and she laughed again after a few seconds. That was when Millicent realized Vinnie couldn't hear or see her father. She was relying on the panther to tell her everything. A panther necromancer?

Millicent took a step back and felt the man behind her before she could disappear.

"Move and I'll hunt you down." Nodding slowly, she closed her eyes. "What does he want here? Or for that matter, what do either of you want here?"

"That's his daughter and my niece. I only came to see if I could talk to her." The man behind her said nothing, and she turned to look at him. It wasn't Steele but the other man, Mitch. And he looked no less scary. "You're going to kill him, aren't you?"

"You too if you fuck with what is mine." He looked at Vinnie as she spoke to her dad, and she did too. "She's my mate. But you never answered me; why are you here? Are you with him, a part of his plan to kill her?"

"He wants the house. I'm not sure what plans he has for it, but...well, I don't want to help him. I might have as a living person, but not anymore. Whatever he wants in that house...he says there is treasure, but I don't know. But whatever he wants with the house, it won't be good for the humans around here." He looked at her, and she could swear he was looking into her very heart. "I don't want to hurt you or Vinnie. I've discovered, too late as it turns out, I want to live a peaceful and quiet life. Or death, I guess. And if...no, when you kill him, send him away, I'm going to enjoy my death much more than I think I ever did my life. I wasn't a nice person."

"My name is Mitch Riley, and you're Millicent Graham." Millicent nodded. "She thinks...Vinnie thinks you're in with her mom and dad on whatever it is they're planning. And that you might try to hurt her or her grandmother."

"I'm not. I have to...I can't not do what he tells me so long as it's not harmful to others. If he wants to me hurt someone I can refuse it, but coming here, to see if I could get in the house, I had no choice but to try. In the event you don't know, I can't." He nodded as if he knew this already. "I can help you. That is if you'll let me. I know that you've no reason to trust me, but I really do want to help."

"Do what?" Yes, that was a good question, and one she didn't really have an answer for. "From what I can see, you're here with him and he's out there now screaming at my future wife to get her to allow him into her home. Why? And since you say you don't know other than this treasure, you're really of no use to me."

"Yeah, I've heard that my entire life." It hurt her that he was right. And worse yet, she hated that she could not go back and change what had passed. But she really did want to help him, help them both. "I could find out what they want the house for and tell you. I mean, I don't know how to tell you anything you might not already know, but I could listen to him when he complains."

"He seems to do that a great deal." Nodding, she told him he did. "What if I did use you to get information? Why do you think I should trust you not to be with him anyway?"

"I don't know. I could tell you that I find I no longer like the man he is. But I'm pretty sure that I was just as bad as he is when I was alive. I could tell you that I have found that I love my niece more than him, but that's not true. I don't hate Vinnie like I thought I did, but he's my blood, dead or not. Amber? I never liked her, but that's not the point, is it?" He told her he was more interested in why they were going to hurt Vinnie. "I don't know that they want to hurt her. The house is all he can talk about. I know for a fact that there are safety precautions that Vinnie put in to keep the two of you safe. Even this, this power that keeps us away, is helping, but as to why he wants in, I really don't know. If there is a treasure and that's what he wants in for, then he's dumber than I thought."

"I think he's trying to get in to kill her." She had no answer for him because to be honest, it would be like him to kill his only child. For no other reason than she was breathing. "Did he say what sort of treasure there was? Physical, or just in his mind."

"Diamonds and emeralds, he told me. Some old money. Mostly, he said it was jewels. I have no idea what he thinks to do with them. He can't even lift them up, much less sell them. Unless that's what he has Amber doing." She thought on it. "Christ almighty, he's using his wife to get into the house to do his dirty work. He'd do it too. And so would she. They have this...they're attached like you'd not believe. He does things and she has always been right there with him. In anything. When they put out the order to kill him, I was surprised that she wasn't brought up on charges as well. But he'd do it. He really would."

"You mean kill his daughter." She nodded and watched as Vinnie laughed again at something her father had said. The panther never moved from her position at her feet. "I'll think about your offer. But if you do hear something and let me know, then I'll talk to Steele. He has more power than I do."

Nodding, Millie felt better than she had in a long time. At least since she'd been killed. She turned to watch the exchange between the two of them as Mitch was when she thought to ask him about Vinnie.

"She can't see us, can she?" He said nothing. "She could if she wanted. I know that Amber could see Horrie when he came around. All she has to do is concentrate hard on him and the rest will be easy. She might not like what she sees, but she'll be safer if she can see us. But I'm sure you know that, don't you?"

"My friend told me the same thing. She has to want to see us and believe in me." She nodded, then turned to him. "What do you see when you look at him? Do you see the monster that I do?"

"Yes. And I see you for what you are as well." He asked her what that might be. "You're in love with Vinnie. And you glow with it. Like Steele does with his wife's love. Use it against him, all of us if you need to, and you'll be as powerful as you can be when you deal with the dead. We do not...most of them don't care for the concept of purity. And you have it with your love for her. That gives you more power than most people have running in their homes...you are in love."

Millie left him then. She didn't want to see him making fun of her. She wasn't sure he would, but things had been so good for her lately that she didn't want to mess it up. Going to see her sister-in-law wasn't always a good thing, but Millie was determined to help Mitch and Vinnie if it was the last thing she did. And for some sad reason, she thought perhaps it might be.

Chapter 7

The morning had dawned bright and sunny. Of course. But so long as she stood as still as she could and didn't venture into the sunshine streaming into the room, Vinnie figured she could stay long enough to see what the judge was going to do about this ridiculous law suit. And the more she found out about the couple she'd been about to represent, the more she wished she could hunt them down and drain them both. She thought she might yet if things didn't go the way she wanted them to. When the judge came into the room, Vinnie actually smiled. Judge Wilson was a man known for his lack of tolerance for stupid people taking up his time.

"Your honor, my client—" The judge lifted his hand when he picked up the file. She had no idea who the attorney was for the Bruces, but so far he was not doing well. Even new attorneys on the scene knew not to speak before him. Judge Wilson ruled the courtroom. "Your honor, I think that this has—"

"I think you should shut up." Judge Wilson laid down the file he'd been looking over and glared at the younger man. That was another thing that most knew. He did not pretty things up when he spoke to you. It was harsh and to the point. "You're in my courtroom, buddy, and what I say goes. Now. Sit your butt down there and keep quiet until I say you can talk, or I'll bring you up on contempt charges. That's not a way to get on my good side, in the event you didn't get that."

When it looked like he was going to talk again, Roger Pratt, a good friend of hers and a shifter, actually laughed. It turned into a harsh cough when Judge Wilson looked at him, but it was funny to see the younger man to his right squirming in his chair. Things might be okay after all.

"It says here that you're suing Mr. Mitch Riley for loss of wages. That happened nearly ten years ago. You just now figuring out you don't have a job?" The attorney started to speak, and the judge cut him off. "I'm speaking to this here Bruce person, not you. You can have your turn later. For now, I want to know what he has to say about this."

"Sir, I assure you I knew I was without funds coming in. At least not as much as I should have been taking in. I think that we've been passed over a great deal over the years for the more...long term children because of the lies this man told about me and my wife. And that was a loss of wages we're talking about. We were on the verge of calling in his social worker when he called in all those lies about us. And the things he told them, sir, are just not true."

"Things like what?" The judge picked up the file again. When Mark didn't answer him, he asked him again. "What sort of things did he tell on you about? Here, I have the transcript on what he said when Mr. Riley called in. So how about you tell me what you think he said."

"Well, we had to ask him to leave because he was trying to have sex with my wife." Everyone in the room burst out laughing, and that seemed to piss off Mark. "Well, he did. She was a lot thinner back then and much prettier, but he did it."

"Hey." His wife, Carol, slapped her husband on the arm. "You're not right. I've still got it. You sure do want it often—"

"Be that as it may, we're talking about what sort of things that the younger Mr. Riley would have said to the office of child welfare when he called in." The judge actually shivered a little as he continued. "Please do not bring up any of your domestic issues in my courtroom again. I don't have the stomach for it, and I'm sure this courtroom doesn't either. Now how about you answering my question on what sort of things this young man might have said when he supposedly lied about you?"

"Your honor, if I may be permitted to speak, my client is seeking damages not just to his reputation, but loss of wages for all the slander that Mr. Riley has been spewing. There are things said by him, in his comments to the offices, that hurt both my clients when they applied for a larger house loan, as well as on any job application that they tried to fill out to add to their household to help the boys they did manage to care for." The attorney shuffled around some papers, but never handed anything to the judge or anyone else.

"And again, I ask you what you think this boy said about your client." The lawyer started to shuffle the papers around in front of him again. "Not the whole thing, Jefferies, but the highlights. Surely, you can do that without a sheet of paper in front of you. Whatever you have written down there, surely you can tell me some of it."

"He told them that my client beat him and tied him to the bed nightly. It wasn't the first time that this occurred, but it had happened over a period of months and months." He handed the bailiff a file finally. "As you can see here, both my clients needed medical attention when the younger Riley fled the house that night, and it was a couple of days before they were able to make the call regarding him and his behavior."

"They didn't tell the police this?" Vinnie nearly laughed when the judge asked. "I mean, they were right there, I'm sure. Someone would have called this in, am I right? I think I even saw a police report filed by the Bruces. Only it said that...let me look. Oh, here it is. It says here that they'd been set upon by thieves and that they'd had a break-in. Doesn't sound like an attempted rape to me. Does it to you?"

"They were trying to make it easy should the young man want to return." The lawyer was flustered, and he was making stupid mistakes. "Should he want to return, they didn't want the police involved. He was a good boy, after all."

"I'm sure they didn't want him to come back. And when he returned, which I'm to understand that he didn't, what were they going to do to him, or for him? Tell him not to do that again and let it go? From what you just said to me, it had happened before." More fumbling with paperwork. "Jefferies, do you think that those sheets in front of you are going to give you some sort of divine answer? They're not, let me tell you. Ask your client what his plans were for the kid if he returned."

As he sat and began whispering to his client, Vinnie looked at Mitch. He was sitting next to Roger. The two of them were talking as well, but it was more on the game and living with her than anything that was going on in the courtroom. When Jefferies stood up again, they both fell silent.

"They would have gotten him professional help." The judge waited, as did everyone else in the room. Professional help for what, she wanted to ask him. But apparently that was all they were going to get.

"Okay, let me get this straight here. Because, I have to tell you, this one boggles the mind a little." Judge Wilson picked up the file and looked at it briefly before putting it back on his dais with a shake of his head. "Your client is suing Mr. Riley, Mr. Bennett, Mr. Stark, and Miss Graham for loss of wages. I'm not even going to ask how the others are involved. I'm figuring it's a quick buck. But, I digress. They're suing these people for nine million dollars each over lost wages. And the state as well for the same thing. Even though—and this one is the mind blowing thing yet— they not only continued to take in boys to care for them in the foster care system, but they were paid as well. To the tune of nearly seventy thousand a year. For ten years after the young Mr. Riley left their care. Do you have any idea how utterly ridiculous that sounds? Not to mention, nowhere at any time did the kid say a word against the Bruces. Not verbally, nor did he come in and write it all out. He said he'd had enough and would rather take his chances on the street. That's all. So this slander? I think it's something they were maybe feeling a might guilty over and projected. What do you think?"

"My client believes he could have been paid better and had more income had it not been for the leaving of Mr.

Riley." Judge Wilson looked at Mitch, then back at the Bruces as Jefferies continued. The man was completely ignoring the fact there was no basis for their complaint. None. "Because of what he did, they were without the proper funds to have the many luxuries in the house that young men need now, and they believe that is why they were passed over for pay increases over the years as well as some of the other benefits that are afforded to state employees."

The judge leaned back in his chair and looked at the wall to his left. Wilson was a good man with four boys of his own. He had to know how much this was going to cost the state if this went to trial, as well as how it would be looked at in the future. This case did not need to go any further than it had.

"You know what I'm going to do? I'm going to let you proceed with this thing. I think...no, I know that things are going to come out in this trial that are going to turn your hair white." Vinnie had started forward when she noticed Mitch and Steele and how they were not surprised by the judgment. Stepping back a little, she waited to hear what else was going to be said by the judge. "I'll hear this one. It'll be good to know I was able to do something good on the side of justice of the little guy. We'll hear this on...two weeks from today. And Jefferies, I'd suggest that you get your crap together in the meantime. Find out what you're dealing with before it's too late, if it's not already."

Vinnie stood where she was until she knew it would be safe for her to come out of the shadows, when the sun was not so bright in the room. Mitch winked at her and Steele pounded him on the back as he moved to her. There was something extremely sexy about the way her man moved, and she wanted to take him home and show him. The moment he touched his mouth to hers, she decided the house was too far and turned him to the wall. His soft laughter had her grinning up at him.

"As much as I'd like to take you up on the offer you are so deliciously giving me, I think there are too many people around for us to continue this. What do you think?" She nodded, kissing Mitch's neck as he talked, his hands holding her to him tightly. "The judge has a wife, did you know that? She died about six months ago. And they're closer now than before." That gave her pause, and she looked at him now.

"She's been talking to him about this case? And he's...he knows things that he might not otherwise know." Mitch nodded. "What does she know that made him take this...she knows it all, doesn't she?"

"Yes. She's friends with Connie Aster, Steele's grandmother, who wants to meet you by the way. Anyway, she hooked Mrs. Wilson up with a couple of the people that didn't make it out alive, and she in turn told her husband. I didn't think this wasn't going to trial. The judge is going to expose them and what they've done to us."

Vinnie tried to wrap her mind around the fact that the ghosts were going to help her and Mitch. Not that she didn't believe they were out there. It was just that they were not at all like she'd been told as a child. Well, Mitch was getting the most help, but her too. Mitch was called over to speak to Roger, and she leaned against the dark part of the wall. As she stood there thinking about everything she'd been told and what was actually true, she saw someone. As her aunt moved toward her, Vinnie wanted to run and hide.

Please don't. He had no idea that I was coming here. Vinnie looked at Mitch and her aunt laughed. *Not him. He can see me, as can most of the others in this room right now. Your father doesn't know. I wanted to talk to you. I'm glad you can see me now.*

Why can I see you now? Millicent only shrugged. *This is a trick, isn't it? Father is going to come here now and hurt everyone somehow. You're just setting me up so I'll lower my guard or something. I have news for you, I won't let that happen.*

Me either. Vinnie followed her aunt to the chair in the back of the courtroom and sat down when she looked like she had as well. *I was wondering how we could speak in such a crowded room. I suppose we can talk like this because we're blood related. You think?*

Vinnie just realized then that they were talking through a link that had formed between them when she'd turned twenty-five. Her aunt would torment her at night when she'd be out trying to make herself safe, and had on occasion scared her so badly that Vinnie had stayed cowering in her room for fear of being hurt. Her Aunt Millie wasn't a nice person.

I have no idea. Why are you here? Millicent looked hurt, but Vinnie had had enough of her aunt and her ways to last several lifetimes. *If you have a message from Father, I don't want to hear it.*

I think you do…I think you need to. He's going to kill you and Mitch. Steele and the rest of them too if he can get close enough. And having your house is going to make that possible. She asked her how she knew. *I talked to your mother. She told me everything, even things that I'm sure she didn't mean for me to know. I still have the power to command her, which in this case came in handy. Your father and mother are plotting against you and Mitch.*

What does my house have to do with all of this? And the treasure that you told Mitch about. And so you know, there isn't one that we can find. And Hugo and I have been all over the tunnels. Millicent nodded and asked her about the vault, and whether she'd found that one. *No. There is a safe in the office and the one that I have in my rooms, but that's not what you mean, is it?*

No. Somewhere in the tunnel systems is a dead wall. I'm not sure why she's calling it that, but that is what she has in her head. I'm thinking she means false wall, and that you have to know where it is to find it. The wall can be moved, and behind it is a large vault, like you'd find in a larger bank. She showed me a picture of it even. It has one wall that has drawers in it, as well as another wall that has old trunks in it. I'm not sure what are in those, and your mother didn't seem to know either, but they're treasure chests, she calls them. Vinnie asked her what they were going to do with this treasure. *Pay a witch to bring your father back.*

Will that work? Aunt Millie said she had no idea, but he believed it, as did her mother. *And the tunnels. Does he have it in his head that he can use them to get around the city? Or...he thinks he can get into houses this way, doesn't he?*

He knows he can. There are no plans for the house you live in, and up until you banned them from your home, your father was going through all of them looking for where they might lead. Amber said your father would explore the tunnels, then come to her to have her write the information down for him. She has known about this all from the very beginning, and her duty was to make you allow her to live with you so that they'd have all the access they needed. Vinnie asked her why she was helping her. *Because...because I've come to realize that I wasn't a nice person. There was no reason for me to treat you or anyone as I did. And now I find that while it's too late for most of the things I did to everyone, I might be able to help you. That means a great deal to me.*

And I'm supposed to just trust you. Her aunt said she hoped that she would. *I don't know. You are his sister.*

Yes. And you're his daughter, but that does not mean that either of us need to continue, as I have done, in his footsteps. I want to help you. I can help you all. Her aunt stood up. *I'm sorry for everything, Vinnie. You have no idea how sorry I really am.*

After she left, Vinnie went to find Mitch. She needed rest and to think. Telling Mitch she'd see him later, Vinnie moved to her rooms and lay on the bed. Sleep was hard in coming to her.

Chapter 8

Steele watched the doctor as he examined his wife. Kari was really glowing with health, and she was as happy as he was about the baby coming along. When a client came into the room with them, her body clad in an old nurse's uniform from what he thought was the early part of the century, he wanted to tell her to go away for just a little while longer. But Kari touched his arm, and he looked at her.

"Go. Whatever she needs, you have to help her with it." The doctor asked her what she'd said, and Kari told him she was saying Steele was a huge help. When she nodded to the door, he left the room and looked for the nurse. She was standing next to a small child and a very pregnant woman.

Steele's powers, or whatever they were, had gotten a great deal stronger since he'd met and married Kari. He didn't know if it was her or the fact that he was letting them shine through. Whatever it was, he could now speak to clients even if they weren't for any reason able to speak verbally.

"I have something for your grandmother. She asked me to look into some things for her." He nodded and smiled. Grandmother was forever having someone come to him with a bit of this or that. Last week it was a recipe for a Kentucky bourbon cake, which they'd made twice now and eaten every morsel. "It's about young Mitch. And a few others that were at the house."

That got his attention. Mitch had been having a parade of ghosts coming and going for the last several days. It was about his trial, he knew that, but it was scary to think how many of them had been hurt by the Bruce family. Some they had murdered, but quite a few of them had committed suicide rather than live with what had been done to them.

"I know where the files are at the old part of the hospital she said you'd need. Medical records on some of the boys were there. When the hospital turned things over to that new system, those boys that were dead—not just those from that horrid house, but all boys and girls from foster care that were just gone—weren't put there. I guess they were thinking that if nobody claimed their little bodies, there was no reason to put them in the system now." Steele asked her where they were. "There's a back stairs to it from this area. It's been closed off for some time I guess, but you can still get there though the doctor's office. He knows it's there, but never uses it. If you go, take a torch with you, as the power has long since been taken out."

Nodding, he tried to think how he could get into the office without making a scene. But the nurse winked at him and made her way down the hall to the office. Steele followed but didn't enter when she did. As she told him how to get to the doorway, Billy and Carlton showed up.

He didn't even wait for them to explain how they were going to distract everyone, but made his way into the office and the door when the first scream tore through the offices.

The stairwell was dark and quiet. Cobwebs decorated every inch of the wide wooden staircase, but he turned on the flashlight he always had with him and made his way down the steps, using his jacket as a sort of broom to sweep the cobwebs out of his face. At the bottom of the stairs, he paused and looked around. There were more than just files down here. Ghosts were everywhere.

The man that approached him smiled. He'd bet anything the man was from the thirties or thereabout. His mode of dress was a dead giveaway, and the hat he had on was a perfect foil for the pinstriped suit and smallish tie.

"You'd be Steele." He nodded at him. "Been told to expect you. Come along then, we'll get you put to rights with all this bullaballoo." He moved with the man, careful not to let any of the others move through him. He hated that, the feeling he got when they walked through him. The man seemed to understand this and shooed the others back.

"Why haven't they moved on to where they want to go?" The man stopped and looked around as if he just realized that they hadn't moved on when they should have. "There should have been someone to come and help them when they passed away."

The man started walking again, his head bent low like a man who was going to the gallows or something. Steele started to ask him again why they'd not moved, but the man started talking. Steele could hear the sadness in his voice.

"I suppose for some of us, this is better. We get to talk to those that need us. There is a whole floor of people here that can talk to us, you know. They call it the geriatric floor, but we call it the fun floor. I think in a way we might offer them comfort before they pass. Most of them go on now, but we...well, we like it here. We're used to it, I guess." Steele could understand that, he supposed. "There do be a few of us that should have moved on, I guess. Those that just sit in the corner waiting. Don't know what they might be waiting on, but there they wait."

"And you're their keeper of sorts." The man laughed again, and that was when he'd let a little of his hold go on his body. He'd been shot about ten times in the chest and once in the head. He'd not been a good man when he lived, apparently, and someone had made him pay dearly. "How long have you been here?"

"Long time. When I first died, so long ago now that I rarely think about it, I wasn't what you might call a cooperative person. Gave those men and women meant to help me a bit of a bad time of it. They kept adding onto my sentence over and over until I guess I finally got it." His laughter this time was bitter and cold. "I have had more years here than I did living. But I'm making up for it now. I'm sort of an ambassador to this place. Making sure we get what we need, and I even set up this sort of schedule for the dying. You know, matching up them with someone that might have a few things to share with them. It's been working well for us all."

"I want to thank you for that." He waved Steele off, but he knew the man was proud of what he was doing. "When you have a need, something that you can't get, let me know and I'll see that you get it." The man, Conner he said his name was, told him he'd do that.

"This here is what you want. Oh, and Nurse Bessie said to show you the way out. Ain't that pretty, but you'll see sunlight soon enough." Steele nodded as he picked up the first box of files. "The ones you'd be looking for are in there. She said them boys had been passed over. So's you know, two of them are here now." Steele looked around, seeing several young men, as well as a couple of small children. It was sad to think they'd lost their lives so young.

"Can they talk to me?" Conner said he'd ask but not to count on much. When he returned a few minutes later with a young man, Steele knew his name. His file was the first one he'd pulled out. Garth Bell. "Do you know who I am?"

"Yeah, you're that guy who sends us on if we wanna go. I don't, just so you know. I got me a nice gig going here and—" The back of his head snapped forward, and Steele had to cover his laughter with a cough. Conner had been there long enough to know he could tap someone when needed. "He said that I wasn't to bullshit you. That you needed me to help you. What do I get out of this?"

"Years off your sentence if you want it." The boy looked at Conner, then back at him and shrugged. "There's a family, the Bruces. They're suing a friend of mine for running when things got out of hand. I was trying to find something on them so that they won't win."

"Mitch." Steele said that was right and asked him how he knew his name. "'Cause I was there that night. The night he lit out of there like his pants were on fire. Him and this kid by the name of Thomas—let me think on his last name—but they were being tied up when I seen them. I go back there sometimes to just piss them off, but I can't do much."

"When you were there, did you see anything else? I mean...well, what sort of things they were doing to them?" The kid looked around, and then when Conner moved on, Steele waited. There was going to be a story here, and he was sure it was going to be horrific.

"I know what they did to us boys there. Did it to me too until I hanged myself one night. Buried me in the back yard so that nobody would know what they'd done. Not that anybody would have visited my grave anyway, but I just got all wrapped up in a dirty sheet and tossed in the ground." Steele decided he would make sure the boy got what he deserved in the way of a proper grave and marker. "Anyway, I could see they were planning to rape them both. Tied them to the bed with them cuffs, they had. Used them on me a few times too, but now I got me a little power and blasted them right off Mitch. He helped that other boy out when them other two were down. Thomas near tore off that man's dick...penis, and the woman got herself kicked in the face a few times and they was down, let me tell you."

"Were there any more boys after that?" Instead of answering him, Garth looked to his left at the three kids sitting in the corner. They were beaten, not only physically but also in what was left of their minds. "I can help them if they want."

"They killed themselves like I did." Steele asked him what he meant. "You know. We are damned. Not going anywhere but to hell, and if it's all the same to you, I'd just as soon stay here and help out. But those over there...well, I don't know that anybody could help them out any more. They're done. And you know what I mean by that."

He did. Steele had seen it plenty in his life. They were the lost, people who knew they were dead and just simply had given up. They would use up their time in this place by doing nothing but being dead. It would be a long and very painful existence for them. And Steele also knew if they didn't want help, no one would be able to give it to them. But he thought he could help Garth.

Gathering all the files he thought he'd need, Garth and Conner led him to the opening deep within the hospital he was sure hadn't seen a broom or mop in more decades than he'd been living. Turning to the two men, he told them thanks.

"You need me, you know how to reach me. I'm here for you." They both nodded, but he wasn't sure they were believing him. Losing hope was terrible when you were alive, and he'd bet it was horrific if you were dead without it. "I'd like to be able to call on you should I need you. Connie said you were helpful to her, and I'd like to see if you'd be willing to help me as well."

"You can count on it. Steele Bennett and his men of justice, they're ones to have in your corner. You just call on either of us and we'll be more than glad to pull a rabbit out of our hats for you."

As Steele made his way to his car, he called Mitch and let him know what he'd found and who he'd spoken to. He could tell he was distracted about something and started to ask him about it when he finally told him. Steele picked up a little speed in his walk then.

"We found the treasure. Steele, it's...holy shit, Steele, it's really a treasure." He could hear Vinnie talking to someone in the background. "You have to come here. I think. Christ, we've hit the mother lode."

~~~

Vinnie watched as the men took more and more boxes out of the vault to be inventoried. She looked over at Luther as he laughed with Connie and Billy. She was sort of a little creeped out about them. Not that they were ghosts, but that she could see them. When Mitch came over and kissed her again, she wanted to hit him as well.

"You're not having fun." She told him she was. "No, you're not. You're about to jump out of your skin. What is it? All the people here?"

"No. They don't bother me. I just...why did he say he had this put in if all he was going to do was put stuff in it? I mean, I know that's what a vault is for, but this is as big if not bigger than any bank vault I've seen." They both looked in the cavernous rooms. "What are we going to do with all of this?"

There were at least four rooms in the large opening. One entire wall was made of drawers from top to bottom, each of them labeled and all of them filled. Diamonds and other stones were in most of the drawers, but there were also watches and cufflinks. Tiaras and earrings. There were more things in just the drawers than there were in the completed stock of any jewelry company. Then there was the furniture.

Roll top desks...three of them. Secretaries that were covered in silk sheets with not a speck of dust on them. Luther told them he'd had the climate control put in even back then, knowing he'd want to keep things nice. Books lined glassed fronted shelves, first editions, most of them signed. Pottery that she knew was as old as her. There were spears and guns, knives and swords. And the most beautiful collection of tea cups she'd ever seen. Hundreds of them.

"I would like to suggest you open yourself an antique store. It's what the missus and I had planned to do. But when she died...it broke my heart and I just never thought of this room again." Luther looked in the rooms and smiled at her. "She so loved the little tea cups, you know? Collected them all over the world. At one time we were going to put them on the market, and they alone were worth millions. Imagine that. Tea cups that are worth more than most people make in several lifetimes. But you should do it. You'd be very good at it."

Connie had told her the same thing. And Vinnie had considered it even then. She had warehouses full of things she'd collected too. Things that she'd used when she was younger. Items that had caught her fancy, books that she'd read. Her collection wasn't nearly this large, but hers with this would fill several stores and then some. When Mitch came back out with another load of things he wanted her to see, she looked deep into the box and saw a key. Picking it up, she asked Luther about it.

"Oh my...I'm embarrassed now. That goes to the warehouse." She asked him what warehouse. "Mine. Well, yours I guess. It was part of the house when I sold it to you. A building and some...well, this will look like nothing in comparison."

"A warehouse. I own...do you think someone might have told me this?" Luther grinned at her and said he had. "When? I think I would have remembered someone telling me I own a warehouse full of stuff."

"I think it was discussed the day you came to the house with your mother. You and she were arguing about your father and aunt, I believe. She asked me where the key was to the warehouse, and I told her that I'd have to find it." He shrugged. "I think I might have met the sun a few days later. It was a very hard time for me, you see. And once the house was sold, I simply joined my lovely missus."

As he moved away and then faded out, Vinnie made her way to her office. There was some mention of the warehouse there, she thought, and she wanted to see just what it said. She knew wording in contracts could be either damning or helpful.

As soon as she pulled out the deed to the house, she read the part where she not only owned the house and the said warehouse, but she also owned the contents. To do with, it said, as she pleased, as they were part and parcel of the house. She looked up when the door opened. Mitch was standing there looking like a man on a mission.

"We own a warehouse. Did you know that?" He told her that he didn't but was glad for them. "Why? Oh, to store this stuff in, I guess you're thinking. Well, that might not work out so well either. Apparently it's full. From top to bottom, and somewhere along the line someone has even gone so far as to purchase the buildings next to it on either side. We have three such places."

"And the plans to open the antique shop, you think that might be a possibility now?" Vinnie told him she thought it might be. "And the things down there, do you have plans for all of it? There are things in there that some museums would love to have if we don't find a need for them."

"If you'd like. The house and everything else I owned before you is now yours as well. If we decide to donate some of the things or sell them, we make that decision together." He nodded and still stood near the door. "Are you coming in or leaving again?"

"I'd very much like to come in you." Her body heated immediately. "However, there is something that I'd like to talk to you about first. I found something in the vault in the sublevels and I asked Luther about it. He told me a very wonderful story. Would you like to hear it?"

"Yes." Her voice sounded hoarse and a little dark. Clearing her throat, she moved her chair back to regard him. "What is it you found?"

"When he and his lovely wife were first together — about four hundred years or so ago, he thought — they were in the south of France visiting a friend of theirs, and he showed them his collection. One part of his collection was a jewelry box filled with things he'd picked up at an estate auction. I guess back then, they had them for families that didn't have the funds to pay for some funeral expenses or a trip." Nodding, she said she'd done the same thing, picked things up. "The man's name wasn't important, I guess, because Luther couldn't recall it. But he did tell me about one piece in particular."

As he made his way to her, she felt her body heat up more. Whatever he had, she knew it was going to be epic. Her mind was running a mile a minute and kept getting sidetracked watching him move. When he was standing next to her, she reached out and ran her fingers down his erection outlined in his jeans.

"You said you wanted to come inside of me." He nodded and dropped to his knees. As he spread her legs wide and moved between them, Vinnie moaned. "This is good. I can almost feel your tongue now."

He took her left hand into his and kissed her palm before sucking each finger into his mouth and then moving to the next one. The longer he suckled at her hand and fingers, the wetter she got. Curling his hand at the back of her head, he pulled her to him and kissed her like he never had before.

It was consuming and giving. Heartbreakingly soft and warm. His breath moved along her cheeks as he lifted his head, and then he sucked her lower lip into his mouth and bit her. Vinnie felt her inner beast move along her skin, her need was so high. But instead of taking her, which she thought he was going to do, he took her hand into his again and slipped a ring on her finger.

"Victoria Alexandra Millicent Graham, would you marry me? Would you keep me safe and love me? Every day will you wake up beside me, lay down by me, and love me? Have children with me, grow older with me? Will you, Vinnie Graham, be my wife for the rest of our days together?"

She looked at the ring that was at her second knuckle. The band was wide, almost half an inch wide, and a gold so brilliantly bright it hurt the eyes. When he rolled it around so she could see the set on it, Vinnie cried, covering her mouth with her other hand.

"It's a Medici. I met him once, Jean-Baptiste Mellerio." The ring...words could not begin to describe the sheer beauty of the ring. "There is a shop, Mellerio dits Meller, in France still. Where they first came to that country. He made jewelry for kings and queens. Wherever did he get this?"

"He said he picked it up from his friend, who would never tell him where he'd actually gotten it. It looks as if it was made just for you." She lifted her hand so that the ruby and diamond could catch the light. "I love you, Vinnie. Will you marry me?"

"Yes." She grinned at him. "But didn't you say something about coming inside of me? I think that would be a good way to seal the deal."

"Take off your clothing for me. Then I want you to get up on the desk so that I can drink my fill of you first." She did as he asked, standing up and started to unbutton her blouse while he pulled his shirt over his head. "I'm going to enjoy this. Eating you while you're spread out on this desk. Taking my time with you so that I can feel you come every time you do. Taste you, the cream that you have when you're aroused or coming. It's more than a man like me could have ever hoped for. And you love me too."

As soon as she was naked, she sat down on the edge of the desk and lifted her legs up so that they rested on the arms of the chair he was now sitting in. His cock was hard, straining away from the dark thick curls at his groin. Curling her toes around his thick shaft, she moved up and down him as he rocked upward. When he asked her to lean back, she did so without hesitation. She needed him to make her come.

She knew she was wet. Her pussy had been dripping since he'd walked into the room. But when he pulled her nether lips apart and blew gently over her clit, she cried out at the enormity of feelings that washed over her. When he suckled at her clit, much like he did at her nipples, she knew she was going to come quickly and hard.

When his fingers entered her, touching off several climaxes at once, she begged him to give it all to her. But he took his time now, sucking at her clit, slowly fucking her with his fingers. As she tried to get more from him, riding his mouth as much as she could, Vinnie cupped her breasts and tugged hard at her nipples.

"You should see you the way I am right now." He fucked her harder with his fingers as he watched her, his tongue flicking over her clit just enough to give her a little climax each time. "You're swollen here, your lips are so delicious with your cream. The thought of being able to drink from you any time I want makes my cock hurt to empty in you."

"Please. Fuck me, Mitch. I want to feel your cock inside of me." He laughed, and she nearly snarled at him when he sucked her clit again, this time biting down just enough to bring her up off the table. As he pushed her back down, she sobbed, begged him to finish her. And when he stood up, she nearly came just from looking at him.

It had cost him to eat her this way, teasing her the way he had. His body was covered in a sheen of sweat; the small triangle of hair on his chest was matted now and she wanted to lick him. Sitting up, she took his nipple into her mouth and bit down, using her fangs to draw enough blood that she could nurse from him this way.

"Christ, yes." He held her to him, his hips rocking back and forth as if he were fucking her now, barely touching her, teasing her so that she was in pain as well. Wrapping her hand around him, she leaned down and took just his crown into her mouth and wrapped her tongue around him. The precum at the tip was as good as anything she'd ever tasted. "You keep that up, and I'm going to come down your throat and not your pussy."

She rolled his balls in her hands as he fucked her mouth harder now, nearly gagging her. When she swallowed, he cried out and she could feel his hot cum sliding down her throat. Then she was on her back and he was standing over her.

"You're making me crazy." His cock filled her, slamming so hard into her that he moved both her and the desk. Pulling back, he plowed into her again and again as he stood over her. His hands dug deep into her hips as he took her. He leaned over her, his mouth an inch from hers, and she nearly came when he told her to open her vein. "I need to taste you like this, when you come for me."

Tearing at her throat, she screamed out her release as soon as he took his first mouthful of her blood. She found his beating pulse with her tongue as she tilted his head for her bite and then bit down hard. As soon as he cried out he was coming again, she let herself go, let her own release take her away. He fell atop her. Vinnie knew then that if the sun were to come up right now, she'd be dead and would die a very happy vampire.

Chapter 9

"All we have to do is wait for them to come out of the house and get enough away from it that we can nab her." Amber nodded. It was the fourth time he'd told her what their plan was. She didn't even bother telling him for the tenth time that this was a stupid plan. First of all, she was just one person to take down her daughter; and secondly, every time she asked about what she was to do about the man should he be with her, and he said he had it worked out. But nothing was ever forthcoming about what he had worked out.

"As soon as she is clear, you—"

"Stop telling me what to do." He took a step back from her anger, and she felt good. But it was short lived. When he hit her with his fist, it first made her sick, but she knew that he'd left something behind when he'd touched her.

The slime, as she'd been calling it, had started yesterday evening. She was in her slumber, her casket closed up and the room dark as night, when she heard something in the room with her. Using a little of her power to turn on the lights, she stared at the thing in front of her and realized with a sudden jolt to the system that he was her mate. And that he was falling apart.

"What has happened to you?" He asked her what she meant, and then he walked in front of her mirror. Of course, there was nothing reflecting back at him, but she got up to go near him. Not to touch him but to get a better view. "Your skin, it's melting. Like...I don't know, like you've been turned into a candle and you're falling apart with the heat."

His hands touched his face, and she watched in horror as his fingers entered his flesh and moved it around like mud after a rainstorm. Amber had to turn away or be sick. She'd never thrown up in her life that she knew of, and she wasn't about to do it now.

"You're going to fuck this up." Amber turned to him now, shielding her mind at how badly he was looking as the night wore on. He'd told her he felt no different than he had before, but she could see it. He was going to be a puddle soon, and she'd be left all alone.

"I'm not going to mess it up. And I really hate that word. Use something else." He laughed at her. That was another thing she hated, when he laughed at her. "I'm to stop the car when it gets to this point, and then I'm going to try and see my daughter. If she'll see me. Which I doubt. She's not returned any of my calls for days now. And even when I try to contact her, she's blocked me. It's like hitting a hard solid wall of nothingness. I don't know how this is going to work either."

"If you make this look good, then she'll stop for you." When she asked him what he meant by that, he only told her to do it. The man's lack of help in this was going to make her stake him. If she even could. "Have you heard from my sister?"

"Millicent?" He asked her what other sister he'd be talking about. "I don't know, Horatio, maybe you have in your head that she and I have luncheons together if we could, or we're the best of friends. Or perhaps you've mistaken me for given one bit of concern for the woman who hates me as much as I do her."

"Then I will take that as a no. I wonder where she's off to. I know she wants in this house as much as we do." She asked him why he'd think that. "Well, she sure has been asking me a lot of questions about what we're going to be doing once we were inside."

"She asked me too." He nodded, but Amber thought that perhaps Millicent had another plan in place. "Do you think she means to kill me off once we're inside?"

"And why would we do that? You're the only one that is alive enough to move things around for us. We need you to sell off the stuff for the cash." Well, she thought, that hurt. "And who will help us kill Victoria once we're in the house? You have to do it, Amber. You're the only one that can."

The car coming down the drive kept her from replying. There was plenty to say too. Why was she doing all the work? What were they going to do with all these riches once they got them? Who was she supposed to contact to sell them? Things like that were questions she'd been asking Horrie for days now, and all she ever got in response was that he had it under control.

"What does that say on it?" The van, a big white one with lettering on the side, zoomed past her before she could step out to get it to slow. There wasn't even time for her to see who was driving the thing, much less try to get inside of it to get her daughter. "Did you read what that said?"

"Yeah." She turned to Horrie to tell him what it said. "It's an appraiser. What do you suppose she wants one of them for, unless she's found your treasure? You think that's it?"

Amber looked up at the big house, and her anger doubled at her daughter, and her envy for all the things that Vinnie had that she didn't. A lovely house, servants, as well as her familiar. Amber had lost hers years ago when in a fit of hunger, she'd taken more than she should have from her and she'd died. And there had been no one to replace her with. The only reason that didn't come back to bite her in the butt was because she'd not died at her hands, but the taxi that had hit her when she'd staggered away from her. Stupid woman. What was she supposed to do, go hungry? No way.

"You said she'd never find it. You told me it was hidden so deep in the walls that there was no...Luther." Her temper got the better of her when she thought of the man again. "He told her, didn't he? Showed her where the safe was and then how to open it. Why, the nerve of the man, giving away our money."

Amber stomped around the grassy area she'd been hiding in since the sun had gone down. Luther had betrayed her. Amber looked over at Horrie when he said nothing. But he was gone, and she called for him three times before she realized he'd just up and left her again. Making her way to the end of the drive and where she'd left her car, she was cursing up a storm when a man was suddenly in front of her. She knew who he was even before he opened his mouth to tell her.

"I'm Mitch Riley. And you need to go away and leave us alone." She was so shocked by his statement that when he laughed at her, she lost her temper again. But before she could touch him, reach out and snap his little human neck, she was pinned against a tree hanging from her daughter's hand. Amber tried to think what she needed to do now.

"Vinnie, where have you been, child?" Vinnie shook her hard, and she felt her teeth snapping together. "This is no way to treat your mom. Put me down this minute and let's go up to your house and talk."

"No. I don't think so. I've found I like you not being there." She asked her why she was being that way. "Because, Mother dear, I know you and Father are plotting against me. To take my house and the contents. You're not going to, just so you know. I have things set up nicely now, and I'm not in the mood to have you snooping around anymore."

Her mind nearly shut down. How the heck had she figured it out? But she knew that if she messed up now, Horrie would never forgive her. Smiling as best she could, trying to make her face softer around the feeling of being pissed off, she patted Vinnie's hand and spoke softly.

"I don't know what you're talking about, dear child. Your father is dead. Remember? You staked him out while I stood there and watched you. Now he's gone." Vinnie shook her again. "Stop that right now. I don't know where you get off thinking you can treat me this way, but I will not stand for it."

"But killing me was going to be all right with you, right?" Amber said nothing because she wasn't sure what to say. "And so you know, the money, the treasure that you've been trying to get at? It's not here anymore. I've had it moved to a safer location."

"All of it?" Horrie was going to kill her, Amber thought. "You can't have done all that. And...and...and I don't know what you're talking about anyway. What treasure?"

She was put down, but she wasn't let go. Mitch stood there watching her, and Amber felt like a bug on the end of a pin. It was on the tip of her tongue to order him to go away, but to be frank, she was more afraid of him than she was of her daughter.

"Why are you here, Mother?" When Vinnie asked her again why she was there and where her father was, she snapped.

"What do you need with a house like that for anyway? And the money. You have more than most vampires twice your age have. Why did you have to go and move it all? Your father is going to be mad, and I'm not going to take it from him either." Vinnie just stared at her with that look on her face that Amber had come to hate. "Don't look at me like that. I tried to do this nicely, asking you if I could move in with you when your father died. But you'd not have anything to do with it or me. Why not? And now that he's back and wanting something that I can't give him because of you, I'm going to be the one to pay the piper. As usual. Why are you doing this to me?"

"I don't trust you." Amber slapped Vinnie on the cheek before she could think she should have reigned in her temper a little. But the smile Vinnie gave her in return made Amber's blood run cold and fear wash over her nothing like she'd ever had before. "Do you feel better now, Mother? Did it make you feel like you might, for once, be a parent to me? You haven't been. Neither you nor Father were in my entire life. And the last years, the years after he was dead, I found myself thinking that you were the dumbest person I knew."

"How can you treat me this way? I'm your mother. I gave birth to you." She looked at Mitch, hoping, she supposed, for something from him. "Do you see this? Do you think she won't treat you the same way when she tires of you? She will. Victoria is the most selfish person I know. Like when the money ran out? Her father and I had nothing, and she just wouldn't lift a hand to help us out, ever."

"Perhaps you should have thought of that before you tried to have her killed." She asked him what he was talking about. "Millicent has been most helpful in a lot of things. And if you're thinking of making her pay for this, she's moved on. And happily too. But she told us of the time you left your daughter out in the weather hoping that some human would come along and kill her. Or the time that you dropped her over the side of the bridge hoping to drown her. She was eight and had, thankfully, taken lessons to learn to swim before that incident. Then there was the time—"

"That's not fair. She was a drain on our resources. Do you have any idea how many plans we had to change when she was growing up? Finding someone to watch her was a chore as well. People saw our house and decided that they didn't want to be there, didn't have any desire to even enter our house." His comment had her looking at Vinnie again. "You told him we never mowed the lawn or cleaned up? Why would you...? You should have done that on your own if that's what you wanted. I had no time for such things. Why should we have to keep up our home like the humans do?"

"Because when you live in a human world, they expect you to abide by their rules. Go figure." Slang. Amber barely understood her only child when she spoke English. But when she spoke the things that were well over her head, Amber wanted to hit her. Much like she did her father all the time. "You aren't getting into our home, Mother. You'll never be able to break the spell that's around it, and more importantly, I'm not going to help you or Father in any way. I can see him now, and I'm no longer afraid of what Mitch and the others can do."

"You ungrateful child." Before she could say much more, her mother appeared. That was another person she was sick of, and she wasn't going to take her crap anymore either. "I'll have you know I'm not going to take your criticism anymore either. You've tried to make me feel bad my whole life, and I will not take it anymore, Mother. Never. To me you are dead."

"Oh, that's perfectly fine with me, Amber. You might find it hard to believe, but I wrote you off long ago." Amber was shocked and it must have shown on her face. "What did you expect, Amber? For me to bow down before you and beg you to let me be in your life? No, I'm too old and too set in my ways to ever do such a thing. Especially for a child like you. And in the event you think to come to my home and try and steal what I have there, you'll be out of luck there as well."

"Why? Have you found someone to put a spell on the house that will keep me out? It won't work on your home, Mother. You've already invited me in. In fact, Horrie and I have been going in and out of there for weeks now." Her mother simply smiled. "Are you going to tell me to stop doing as I please? Do you really think you can?"

"I don't live there any longer." Amber told her she lied. "I don't lie, and I have moved out. The house no longer belongs to me, so your entrance privileges have been revoked as of eight tonight. Just as you were leaving the house with that horrid man you married, the house changed hands and the new owner won't be letting you in. Just so you know."

"You can't do that. Why are you doing this to us? We don't have any place to go." Her mother only smiled at her, and Amber turned to Mitch. "This is all your fault. Why did you have to come into our lives and mess things up for us? We had it all worked out, and now it's all messed up because you couldn't keep it in your pants."

The man laughed at her. Not one of those soft kinds of laughs that made you smile, but he threw back his head and roared with it. Birds left the trees over them. Even bugs and other creatures of the night scurried away from the sound, and all she could do was stare at him.

"You think you're insulting me? Not a chance. I'm in love with Vinnie and think the world of her grandmother. And yeah, it took me a while to figure out what I was feeling for Vinnie, but now I can think of nothing but loving her. And we're going to have children together too. Raise them up to be loving and kind. They'll know they're loved too." She snorted at him. Things like that just didn't happen to her kind. "You won't be able to see them, however."

"Like I'd ever want to. Having my own was bad enough. To touch another one now? No, thank you very much." She looked at her mother when she tisked at her. "You said having a child would change me. You said that having a baby of my own would make me happy. Well, you didn't tell me the half of it. Yes, it changed me. Took away my free time. Made it so I could no longer come and go as I pleased. And worse yet, she went on believing that I liked her. Never. Not one day of her entire life. And when she killed my husband and mate, I knew then she was going to die by my hand."

The pain took her breath away. Amber looked down at her chest and touched the wooden spike coming through her left breast. When the burning started, making her dizzy and weak, she turned to see who would have done such a thing to her and was startled to see her mother standing there.

"You should know that I have the full permission of the council to do this. Crimes against your own kind. Theft from your own family. Murder. Death of a human without cause...the list is long, Amber, and you are paying for your crimes."

Amber couldn't speak. There wasn't enough air in the world, much less her lungs, to draw even a short breath. As she fell to her knees, the flames burned the spike enough that it fell to the ground, the fire going out on the damp grasses almost as soon as it touched it. But the fire in her, the burning up of her body, wasn't going to be so easy to quench. Just as she felt her mind explode with more pain, she saw her daughter smile at her. Then there was nothing more.

~~~

"When the time is right, you'll have to kill my mate as well. I've been thinking that she's going to be —" He knew what it was as soon as he felt it. Stake through the heart. As he fell forward to his knees he held his breath, hoping he'd be able to get out of this house before he was —

"Are you all right?" Horrie looked at the man he'd been working with. The man who was going to get him into the house no matter what. "You hurting or something? Way you fell there, I thought for sure that you'd been hurt. But the dead, we don't get hurt. We can get gone but not hurt. You ever heard tell of a man named Bennett? Him and his men, they'll run you off faster than a zipper can come down in a whore house. Been hearing about them men of his for —"

"I'm not sick. I've been staked." The man — Rudy, he thought his name was — only shook his head at him. "I swear to you, I thought for sure I'd been staked. Right through my heart."

"Nah. Maybe you have some indigestion. Never heard of it happening to those peoples like us, but you never done know about some dead." Rudy looked him over both front and back. "You don't appear to have no meat on you. You thinking that something hit you real hard like?"

"No, a *stake*, not a *steak*."

"That clears things up," Rudy said sarcastically.

"You know, a wooden spike through my heart kind." Ruby told him he done don't have a heart now...it took him several seconds to work that one out, and when he did he asked if that was true.

"Sure enough it's true. What you have a need for a heart fer? You can't die from it. Got no reason to be pumping that red juice through you no more. I'm thinking that you just got yourself a little pain, that's all. I think they call it phantom or some shit like that." Ruby laughed again. "We being a phantom and all and getting some pains like that is sort of funny. Don't ya think?"

He rubbed his chest as he stood up. Horrie knew that he'd felt it. Still did. But he was feeling hollow now, like something important had happened and it had torn a hole in the fabric of his being. As Ruby continued to tell him what he had planned for the house, Horrie realized what it was.

"My mate." Ruby told him he had it down to kill her as well. "No. I think she's dead. I think...I think someone killed her."

"Afore me? Well, if you had somebody else doing it fer you, you should have done told me. I got to rearrange my whole strategy now." Ruby shook his head and just started cussing. "You have any idea how much I been looking forward to that? Killing me a vampire would have been great, don't you know."

"Well, you can go ahead and kill my daughter if you want." He nodded, but didn't look none too pleased with that. "She's a vampire too, you know."

"Yeah, but that mate of yours was older. Much older." Horrie wanted to point out that being the mom of his daughter that was the only way it would work, but didn't. The man looked really depressed. "I'll do it, but like I was telling you, I'm going to have to do it my way. No hurrying up for me. I take my time."

"Yes, of course, you'll take your time." As the ghost faded away, no doubt to go and find him something pornographic to watch, Horrie reached out for his mate and felt nothing. Not a soft connection. Not even a wall, but nothingness. He knew then that she'd been murdered.

"My daughter had something to do with it, I don't doubt either. Money grubbing whore. Taking up with those necromancers and now look at her." Three ghosts appeared in front of him, but Horrie didn't bother moving. They were not anyone he had a beef with, and as soon as he stood up, he knew they'd be on their way.

"Horatio Mower Graham?" He nodded. When someone or even in this case, something said your full name, you had no choice but to listen up and tell the truth. "We're here to inform you that your wife and mate, Amber York Graham, is deceased. Staked through the heart. By order of the council."

He waited for them to say more, at least tell him the name of the person who had done the deed, but they only stared at him. When it was apparent that they weren't going to speak until he did, Horrie shrugged.

"What is it you want me to do about it?" They looked at each other, then at him again. "I'm assuming one of you guys did it. Well, thanks. Saved me having to find someone that could do it for me. She gonna be coming here at some point? You know, to spend her days with me?"

"No. She's gone, sent on to where she needed to go to bother us no more." He nodded. Figured she'd do something like that. Just up and leave him to be alone with his own plans. Now how the hell was he going to get into the house without her body to do some of the real work? "You have nothing more to say?"

"Not that I can think of." He pretended to think on it then snapped his fingers. "Oh yeah. My daughter, is she dead yet too? That's the one I really want to have a piece of. No sending her over without a farewell from her daddy dear."

"Victoria has joined the Justice team of Bennett." He felt his body run cold. She did what? "She and her mate have made some considerable donations as well. To the library as well as some of the museums that are around the world. You should be very proud of her."

"No. I'm pissed if you want to know the truth. She took what was mine, and now she's just giving it away like she don't have a care in the world." One of them asked if she'd really stolen from them. "No. But that crap in that safe was mine. I want it and as her dad, I think it should come to me, not get donated to some place where it won't earn me a dime."

"What need would you have for money? You do know that you are dead, don't you? And not taking very good care of yourself either, if you don't mind my saying." He asked him what he meant. "You've not been resting properly. Have you even once been back to your place of death to rest? You can only get rejuvenated there. No amount of rest elsewhere will do the same for you."

"I was staked out in the sun by my own flesh and blood." The men looked at each other then back at him. "You want me to go back there and lay down on the earth and rest? What if someone comes along and finishes the job and sends me over?"

"Sends you to where, Mr. Graham? You have amounted quite a few years onto your sentence here. I do not believe, unless you are zapped over, you'll be going anywhere so that you'd have anything like that to worry over." They all laughed. "You will soon be nothing more than matter that will only stick to someone's shoes if you don't rest soon. Why have you not consulted your book to see what to do?"

"I made the guy take that stupid thing back. I can't read anyway." He told him it would talk to him should that be necessary. "Yeah, so they said. And what do you mean, my sentence? I served up my time when my daughter killed me."

"She had the permission of the council to do that, I believe. It was a case that was heard some time ago, and she fulfilled her promise of making the event happen." Event? His death was an event? Not fucking likely. "As for the things you think should belong to you, I'm afraid that is not going to come to you either. You are, as I have said, dead."

"I fucking know that I'm dead, damn it. Why does everyone have to keep telling me that? I'm not stupid, you know?" None of them said anything, but he could see what they were thinking. "What the fuck do you want, anyway?"

"We have come to inform you that Steele Bennett's man, Mitch Riley, has asked to zap you over, and we have told him he has our permission." Horrie felt like they'd staked him too. "That is all."

Then they just left him. Horrie was suddenly terrified.

Chapter 10

Vinnie didn't care for the way things were going in the big building. People were running around like they had a clue what she wanted, and since she really didn't know, they didn't fucking know either. Finally, she put her fingers in her mouth and whistled. Every person in the big building stopped and turned in her direction.

"I don't want anyone to touch another thing." Several people leapt back from the pieces they were near, and a couple even set the pottery or whatever piece they had in their hands down on the floor. "Good. Now. I know that we have to inventory all of this, but the way we're doing it isn't working out. I know for a fact that several pieces are on several different lists. It's either furniture or it's not. There cannot be a list for desk, office equipment, and wood."

"Good for you." Her grandmother patted her on the back as she stood up as well. "We would like for all furniture to be put over there, the pottery items here, and the crystal there. Any and all jewelry will need to be brought to us and we'll inventory it."

"Thanks." Her grandmother just smiled at her. "What am I going to do with all this stuff? I can open several shops and never put a dent in all the pieces here and in the house. I shudder to think what might be in the other buildings."

"You'll do fine with it. And did I tell you I have some things I'd like to get rid of as well? Since I've sold the house, young Landon has decided that he wants some of the pieces but not all. He abhors the dining room things. In fact, I told him I did as well."

"Beth is going to let me put some of her art in the shop as well. And apparently Addie is selling off most of her parents' things as well. She called them stuffy. I think she's going to come and see what she wants of this too." Grandmother nodded and took the first of what Vinnie knew would be many boxes of jewelry. "That attorney for Steele, he said we'd have to keep track of all these pieces in order to make it easier at tax time. Owning all this free and clear, he said, doesn't mean I won't have to pay taxes on it when it sells. I guess...do you suppose I'll be able to move any of this?"

"I'm to understand that Hugh is going to help you out with putting the things online to sell as well. That will help, I think. Even if they want you to hold it for them so they can pick up some of the pieces, he said he'd make sure that they paid up front. And I think you'll do very well. People love old things. Look at us." Vinnie hugged her grandmother to her. "I've been wondering how you'd feel about what I did."

"I'm glad you took charge, Grandmother. I would never have gotten through this..." She stopped talking when her grandmother shook her head at her. "What do you mean then?"

"Your mother." Vinnie thought about seeing her mother die. The stake coming through her chest as it, too, burned up. "Staking your mother, I mean. That, I'm sad to say, wasn't as hard to do as I thought it would be. She...her mouth was spewing such things that I think it hurt me that she was hurting you so badly. You have to know it was going to be easier for me to do than you. And I know you told the council you'd take care of it. Killing one parent for the good of us all was more than you should have been asked to do."

"I'm actually glad that she's gone. I know that sounds horrible, but it's not like we were very close. I mean...I can't even remember the last time I spoke to her where she wasn't asking me for something, begging me to do something for her or to give her something I had. My house...I can see where she'd want to live there. I guess. It's nicer than hers had ever been. Of course, she never tried very hard to make it so she had nice either."

"Your father and mother were the most selfish people I ever had the misfortune to be related to. Most of the time I would ignore her just so that I'd not have to listen to her tell me what she didn't have. And how she'd never get it. I swear to you, they were old enough to have been able to save fortunes, but they never even tried. Why would you have an electric bill that is well over a thousand dollars a month when you are not using it? They were gone most of the night time, and why burn it during the day when you are at rest?"

They sorted through some of the nicest things she'd seen so far before she answered her. There were times when her bill would come in for a little less than thirty dollars a month. Hugo used little when he watched over her. And Gilda didn't live with them. There wasn't any need for a phone, she had no heat bills to speak of, and no credit cards. The house had been paid off for a very long time and her taxes were paid monthly, which was little compared to what the house gave her monthly. Food wasn't a real issue since she never ate, and Hugo ate whatever he could find in the woods behind them. Most of the time, he would have a deer dressed out and eat on that for several days.

She realized she was color coding the earrings when her grandmother laughed at her. Vinnie had always been organized. She thought perhaps it was because of the way she'd grown up. Chaos was hard to thing for her, and she'd made sure that at least her living space had been clean and things put away.

"I have a lot of money." Her grandmother told her she knew that. "No. I mean a great deal of money. I've been watching markets for a long time, longer than most investment companies have been around. I have stock in businesses that have been around for hundreds of years, which I bought for pennies a share. Now it's worth millions. I was on the ground floor to a great many projects that paid off, as well as a few that didn't pan out as well as we'd hoped. Like you, I've saved and saved, but now...well, with Mitch, I find I want to do things with the money. I'd like to travel, I think. It's more possible today with planes and such than it was when I was younger."

"Then you should do it. I have traveled a great deal and seen things that are still a wonder to me. I don't fly. There is something so confining about that, but I do take ships. You can see so much from the ground. And if I have troubles, I can always leave. I gained that power long ago." Vinnie asked her if she traveled that way as well. "Only if I feel a need to get away. You do know that Mitch can do that as well? You'd have to keep track of him for a little while, but he can travel the same way you do."

"He heals faster already. Much faster than I thought him to." She picked up a pair of ugly earrings and set them aside. She knew they were expensive, but she didn't want them in front of the new showcase. "Also, I can see the clients, as he calls them. I didn't...there are more than I dreamed there would be."

"There is a lot of meanness in the world." Her grandmother picked up the earrings and put them to her ears. "I think I'd like to purchase these. I think them to be quite lovely."

They worked through most of the night. The workers, most of them shifters or other vampires, left one by one until around sunrise, they were alone in the building. Vinnie was moving the things to the safe that had been there when she'd opened the doors as her grandmother moved to see what sort of progress was made on the other items. Just as she turned off the light to leave with her, she saw her father.

He wasn't near enough for her to see well, but she could see that something had happened to him. His face looked like he'd had a stroke—part of it was sagging badly—and his hair had fallen out as well. Her father had always been a very vain man, and to see him like this was a great shock. Telling her grandmother he was there, she told her to move along without talking to him. She was nearly ready to do that when he said her name.

"They told me that you can see me." She didn't say anything but did keep her grandmother close at her side. "I want you to talk to me, damn it. I'm your father."

"Are you? I thought perhaps you'd forgotten that when you thought to have me killed in my own bed. Why is it you and Mother only remember that when you want or need something from me?" He told her to shut up and listen to him. "No. I don't think so. I'm finished with you and whatever plans you want me to be a part of."

"I don't have anything. And if you remember correctly, you murdered me first." She didn't speak. It was obvious, even to her, he didn't have anything. "I want you to take me in. Let me...I don't know, haunt your house so I can have a place to rest. That guy, he said I'd have to go back where you murdered me to rest, but I figure it'll do me just as good to rest where you are so I can shit on you every day."

"Yeah, that makes it so appealing to me. No, you're not going to come to my home. I have a mate now, and you are not going to be anywhere he is. Much less Grandmother." He asked her what that meant. "She's living with me now. She sold her house."

"That fucking bitch. She should have given it to me. Damn it all to fuck and back, won't no one do what's right for me? I tried to go back there to rest and I couldn't get in it any more than I could your house. What did you do, have one of them witches put you a spell on it? Tell me which old broad did it and I'll have a talk with her." She told him who had done it. "You're in cahoots with the necros now, are you? I heard you were mated to one. Your dearly departed mom, she was really disappointed in you."

"I don't care. I could care less what either of you ever thought about me." He just snorted at her, and when her grandmother told to her ask him something, she did. "What were you going to do with all my money, Father? You don't have any needs...you're dead."

"Mother fuck, is that all anyone can fucking say to me? I fucking know I'm dead. But I still have needs, don't I? I have rights too, and you as my kid are going to give them to me." Vinnie had had enough and started for the car that she had gotten a few days ago. "Where the hell are you going? I didn't give you permission to leave me yet. Where is that boy?"

She started to ask him if he meant Mitch, but she saw the other ghost coming toward her. She knew in that moment he was with her father and he'd hired him. Putting up her hand, she stopped him in his tracks.

"Do you know my mate?" The man in front of the group shook his head and told her he didn't care. "He works with Steele Bennett."

"Fuck. No way." Vinnie told him there was a way and he did indeed work with him. "He only told me to kill you. I can. I've been hanging around for some time now."

"You do and I'm going to zap you." The man backed up until he was a few feet from her now. He looked over at her father and then back at her. "He knew that too. I think he meant for you to be zapped as soon as you killed me. It's the way he does things."

The man turned to her father. There was a circle around the man, red hot and all over him from head to toe. Aura, Mitch had told her...they all had them, but few could see them like others could, like they could. When he started toward her father, she moved her grandmother to the car. It was time to leave. As soon as Grandmother was in the car, Vinnie turned to see what was going to happen.

"You done did this to me." Her father, always a stupid man, told him he might want to think about his head getting his ass in trouble with him. He, Horrie, told the man that he was powerful. "Powerful, are you? I don't think so, and the fact that you did this to me...you had me come on out here to do the dirty work, and to hell with the fact that I might get myself zapped."

"So?" The fiery circle around the man burned brighter, and either her father couldn't see it or didn't care. "Like you've been telling me for days now, I'm dead. What do I care what happens to the others now?"

Her father shot back from the blast that had been aimed at him from the other man. It was something that Mitch had told her today. You could protect what was yours if you were dead, but otherwise you had to behave yourself. Three ghosts showed up as her father was being blasted again. This time, Vinnie got in her car and went home. Whatever happened to him now was out of her hands forever.

~~~

Mitch was in the kitchen when they came in the house. It was later than he'd thought she'd be coming home, but the moment he saw her face, Mitch knew Vinnie had had something terrible happen. When her grandmother left them alone, he pulled her into his lap.

"Tell me." She shook her head and told him it didn't matter. "But it does. Something happened and I want to know. I want to help you."

Vinnie let out a long breath, and he wasn't sure she was going to answer him. But when she did, he had to wait before speaking.

"Some men showed up just as the hired killer my father got to kill me figured out that you and I are mates. The man was blasting Father against the wall." He nodded. "Oh, and you should know that Grandmother and I spoke. She's going to take whatever she wants in the way of jewelry to compensate for the sale of her things. I hope we can sell her stuff for her."

"Me too. But back to this man zapping your father. He was a ghost?" She nodded and leaned back on his chest. "So your father hired another ghost to kill you for him, and this ghost didn't know you and I were mates and part of Steele's team?"

"Pretty much. Will he be able to—whatever it is that they do to the dead—will he end him somehow?" He told her he didn't think it worked that way, but would ask Steele. "Yeah, I doubt it would be so easy. I'd just be too lucky. My father said I was to let him live here with us so that he could haunt me. Like that was ever going to happen even if he was alive."

He was glad she'd not changed her mind about that. Not that he thought she would, but it was nice to know he wasn't going to come to see them. He thought about the letter he'd gotten from the Bruces' attorney that morning.

"They want me to settle. I got the letter from them just before you got here. I think they know they're in the wrong and want me to just pay them off." She asked him if he was going to. "No, this has gone on long enough. And I think I need to have some closure. The trial is in three days. I wish you could be there with me."

"I can for a little while. Do you think it will be an all-day event?" He didn't know and told her that. "I don't think it will. I think that once the judge has this thing going he's going to run it out fast. You told me that he was speaking to his wife about it?"

"Yes. I think that maybe Connie has had a hand in this too. I'm not sure what she's been up to, but she and Aster have had their heads together." He didn't ask them. He was sure whatever it was, it wasn't going to be too terribly helpful. And he also had a feeling he was going to be owing the Bruces rather than just having this go away. It was the way things usually went for him. "I'm about as ready as I can be."

"But you're not happy about this." He shook his head, then realized that she couldn't see him and answered her. "You're not without resources you know. I mean, you have money now, and if you want to pay them off, we can do that."

"But it won't end there. In a few years, less I bet, they'll come back and try this again. And again until we're both drained from it. And they'll continue to watch over and hurt children." He shifted on the chair and thought about the night he'd left. "Steele met that boy that helped me. His name is Garth Bell. We're going to find his body when this is over and bury him in the little cemetery on the property. I hope you don't mind, but I said we'd pay for the marker."

"I think that's a wonderful idea. Will he be able to go there and see it?" He told her he would. "Good for him. And for you. To get to meet the person that saved you that night must be scary and nice. You can thank him, like you told me you wished you'd done all those years ago."

But no one had been there to save Garth, and that saddened him even more. After Vinnie went to rest, he went into the yard to meet with the rest of the men. They were headed out again, this time across the United States. There had been a few scary things going on at a high school out there, and they'd been called in. Ray was heading this one up.

"Nine children have reported seeing some unnatural behavior in the school yard. While they are assuring everyone that it is not of a sexual nature, not one of them has been able to tell us just what is going on. Or they won't...we're not sure which right now. Then a teacher was murdered on the grounds and all hell has broken loose."

They were each handed a picture of the woman as the plane jetted them across the states. "Her throat was cut, and she was also shot several times in the head and groin area. There are some saying that it was to cover a rape, but the man who they have in custody says that not only does he not remember doing it, but he had no idea who the woman was."

"Was she hurting the kids?" Ray told Hugh, who asked, that it had not come up that she had. "But we're not ruling it out then."

"We're not ruling anything out." Ray handed them all a second picture. "This is one of the kids that hung himself a few months ago. There wasn't a note left and so far none of this is really helping his parents or the people closest to him. What they have been able to find in notebooks and such was garbled as well as choppy, very unlike the young man, they're saying. He hung himself on the school grounds using one of the few trees that are in front."

"Did he and the teacher know each other?" Ray told him that it was a small school, and it seemed that everyone knew everyone in some way or another. "What have the parents said, anything?"

"So far they've not been involved in the death of the teacher." Another file. "This will give you all the school transcripts of the young man who hung himself, as well as anything the police found in his room that they took in the form of evidence. I'm not sure what they might have needed his grade school yearbook for, but they took that as well. Nothing has been returned to the parents as yet."

"What is it you think is going on?" No one said anything, and Mitch looked up at Ray when he didn't answer Landon. Ray looked...well, he looked like he might know something but didn't want to say it out loud. Mitch thought that was pretty telling in and of itself.

As soon as they landed, he and Steele went to the house of the boy. Steele wasn't sure this was the way to go, but Mitch had a feeling the kid had something there, but as yet, it hadn't been found. Or the boy hadn't wanted it found. The mother let them in, and Mitch saw Jeremy was there with her.

"I don't know what you might think you'll find here. They took it all from me." Steele nodded and told her he'd work on getting the things back. "The only things I really care about are his letterman coat and his class ring. I know they're not going to honor him at graduation in a few weeks on account of him not really graduating, but I'd like to have them all the same."

Jerry, as his friends called him, sat next to his mom when she started to cry again and looked right at him. He felt the connection right away, and Jerry asked him if he could see him.

Nodding, he pointed to the hallway and to where he thought the bedroom was. Jerry led him down the hall to his room and Mitch closed the door behind him. They might need it to be quiet for a few minutes.

"Do you know who killed the teacher?" He nodded and said he did. "Did you have anything to do with it?"

"No. I only know who did it, not...I don't want him to get into trouble. I think he might blame her...well, he does blame her for me being gone and all, but I'm the one that did the deed...you know, killed myself." Mitch told him he knew that. "He's a good guy. Straight up nice. But Ms. Candlewick, she was not as nice as people thought she was. And now...she's coming around here telling me that we were meant to be together."

"She want you to do anything else?" Jerry went to his window but didn't answer him. Mitch knew how hard it was to admit that something had been done to you. And that the people you trusted most were the ones that did it. "My foster family, they're suing me because when they tried to rape me, I told on them."

Jerry turned to look at him. "She didn't have to rape me, if that's what you're thinking. I wasn't going to have sex with her, not intercourse anyway. But the rest? I was willing. At first anyway. But then she...she had a husband, she said, and there was a problem with him."

"Did she want you to kill him?" As soon as he asked, Mitch knew it wasn't that. And when Jerry shook his head, there was a new kind of dread washing over him.

"He liked to see her fucking someone, she told me. And I was prime to watch. I thought that was all it was going to be. Him getting his jollies while I went down on his wife. I never...we never had intercourse, like I said, but it was close sometimes. But when I got to the house, we had a nice dinner and then...." Jerry looked out the window and didn't say any more.

"Did they drug you?" Jerry nodded, still not looking at him. "When you left the house that night, did you know you were going to kill yourself?"

"No. I sort of just come to that after I was taking the fourth shower that night. I just couldn't get clean, you see. And then I got this text from my girlfriend. She said she was looking forward to us having a wonderful wedding night. It was just too much." He turned to look at him then. "You and Mr. Steele, you can help me, right? I don't want to leave my mom, but I need to...I can't be here anymore."

"We can help you." Jerry nodded and told him about the things he'd hidden. "Can you tell me where they are? It would go a long way to helping your friend. Because you know as well as I do he'll get caught."

"Yeah, I know." It took him ten minutes to get to the box. It held his cell phone, which had never been found, as well as a long note telling why he'd done it and why he couldn't live with himself any longer, and sealed the deal on the teacher's fate. He even had a few pictures on his phone that he'd managed to get of the teacher and her supposed husband right before he'd passed out from the drugs they'd given him.

Chapter 11

"Good work out there," Drew said to him when he sat beside him on the way back home. "How did you know? I mean, I know you can talk to them, but how did you know he'd be at his house?"

"His mom was there." Drew said that wasn't much of an answer. "The boy didn't kill himself at his home where his mom might find him, but out where the teacher would. He wanted her to know, even subconsciously, that it was her fault."

"Yeah, I don't think that was anything she was thinking, do you?" Mitch had to laugh. The teacher, not married and selling sex tapes of the boys she'd had sex with on the Internet, had been really pissed off when she found out that not only was she dead, but all her movies had been taken down, as well as her site. "And to find out that the principal was in on it was really a shocker."

Mitch had read the boy's notes before turning them over to the police. He wouldn't have changed them in any way, but he didn't want the mom to find out anything else that would hurt her. The note he'd written to his mom was just where he'd said it would be, in the drawer where the gun had been hidden in her room. He wanted her to find it in the event she wanted to end her life as well.

"He knew I'd think about it, didn't he?" Mitch said nothing to answer her, but Jerry told him he knew that she had several times. "I miss him so much. Every day it's like getting up in a pool of heavy syrup and to have it clog your every pore and every fiber of your being with every breath. I don't...I love him so very much."

"He loves you as well." She knew what they were now. He and Steele had talked to her at length about Jerry and what he wanted from her. "You're going to do as he asked? You'll make sure that it's done that way?"

"I will. I promise him, I promise them all I will do it."

"You think her case will stand up in court?" Landon asked him. Mitch said he thought so. "I do too. Steele is offering his attorneys up to represent her, so I don't think she can lose this one. And to have her donate all the money she gets from the state and donations is going to go a long way to get help for everyone they affected in this."

The foundation that Steele had had his firm set up had already hit its goal of five million. That was hit about ten minutes after the information had been put on the news with the foundation's address. The money was going to go toward setting up a manned suicide hotline, as well as a scholarship fund for the high school. And the assistant principal had given not just Jerry's diploma to his mother, but had presented her with his tassel and cap that the school usually gave to all their honor students. And any more money that was won in the suit was going to be added to it.

"Steele said that you and he have added to it as well. I think that's great of you guys. I'm going to as well as soon as I get home." Mitch told him that was nice of him, and Landon said nothing. "How are you liking the new home?"

"Great. It's a big house. A lot bigger than I thought it was when she suggested I buy it. And I think she really gave me a deal." Landon laughed. "Okay, she gave me one hell of a deal. One buck. That's it, just a buck. She said I was doing her a favor by taking it because of Vinnie's parents and all."

"I guess she's making the same offer to Drew as well. She wants to downsize and getting rid of a few homes to this family is a good way to start. Hugh said he's fine where he is living in the big house." Landon lay back and closed his eyes. Mitch knew he wasn't sleeping. The man never turned off as far as he could see.

"I'd like to ask you a personal question."

Mitch told him to go ahead. "But just so you know, I might not answer you. Or if I do, it's going to be honest and no holding back."

"Did they rape you?" Mitch looked around. He wasn't sure who might hear him, and thought perhaps that was why Landon had come back to where he was and not asked him when they were all there. "The reason I ask is, you had an immediate and profound attachment to the kid. I know from the transcripts he was raped. So I wondered if it had happened to you."

"Yes." Landon nodded but didn't look at him. He didn't even open his eyes. Mitch waited for him to say something. Like, did you like it? Was it good for you? But he should have known better. Landon wasn't that sort of man. None of them were.

"When I get my house finished in a few weeks, I'd like to have you and Vinnie over. To sort of help me break the house in. I know she doesn't eat food, but you do, and I'd really enjoy having you over." Mitch asked him if he could bring Alexandra. "Sure. I like the woman. She's sort of...I guess you could call her old world. And I enjoy talking to her."

Mitch wondered if he was ever going to say any more about his answer. But the longer they sat there talking, the more relaxed he became about not having to explain what had happened. When the plane landed about an hour later, Landon stood up and stretched, putting out his hand to shake. As soon as he took it, Landon started talking in low tones.

"When I was nine years old, my parents sent me to a boarding school. It was nice and I had a really big room. You see, I came from money. A great deal of it too. But my parents were distant, cold. So I acted out, stressed out about everything." Mitch nodded, waiting for more. "Three months after I was sent there, I set fire to my very nice room. It caught quickly, much faster than I ever could have imagined. The building was coming down within an hour of me starting it."

"How many?" Landon nodded but said nothing, still holding his hand. "You set a building on fire, and I'm assuming that someone was killed."

"Two people. However, not from the fire but from trying to save the coke lab they had going in the adjacent building. In their haste, they set fire to their work area and killed themselves. That was the first time I had to deal with a ghost." Mitch knew there was more, but the longer they stood there holding hands, the more worried Mitch got. Then when Landon spoke, he wanted to hug his friend.

"Nothing in this world can bring them back. And even though I didn't directly cause their deaths, I was as responsible for it as if I'd put a bullet in their heads. I'm telling you this because there is no amount of worrying over something that is going to make the problem go away. Money won't solve it, nor will trying to reason with it. It is what it is most of the time, and just letting things ride, letting them work themselves out, is the best way to get it solved."

"You're talking about this thing with the Bruces." Landon said he was talking about everything. "I don't understand."

"You do. You just are too afraid to let it go. This thing with the Bruces, are you doing everything you can? Have you absolved yourself of causing it?" Mitch said he had. "Then there is no reason for you to think it won't work out. Karma is a bitch."

Mitch stared at his friend, and when he let go of his hand and turned to pick up his bag, Mitch stopped him from leaving with a touch of his hand on his arm. Landon looked at him but said nothing.

"Do they haunt you, Landon?" Landon nodded. "Bad? Is it really bad? I can help you, maybe."

"No. You can't help me with them. No one can. They are my...I guess you can call them my penance. Whatever you call them, they're my responsibility, not anyone else's." Mitch wasn't sure that was right and told him so. "Let it go, Mitch. All of it. Lean back, let the rest flow over you, because there isn't shit you can do about it."

After he left him standing there, Mitch thought that Landon wasn't letting it go either. And that his relaxed, laid back appearance was just that, an appearance. Mitch didn't think his friend was following his own advice and letting things go either.

Tomorrow he was going to face down his own form of torment, and for some reason, he had a feeling it was going to be much better than he'd thought. Getting his gear, he stepped off the plane just as a long limo pulled up. When Vinnie stepped out of it, Mitch thought his day could not get any better than this.

~~~

Mitch smiled at her when he saw her. He was the most handsome man when he did that, especially when it was directed at her. As soon as he was close enough, he picked her up in his arms and kissed her. Vinnie felt all melty inside.

"I love you." Her heart skipped several beats when he said it to her. Hearing it from this man was the greatest thing she'd ever heard, and she wanted to treasure it. "I love you with all of my heart and soul. You are and always will be the greatest thing in the world to me."

"I love you as well." They both got in the car, and she started to sit across from him when he pulled her onto his lap. Her legs were on either side of him, and she could feel his hardening cock. Rocking over him, riding him through their clothes, she started to unbutton his shirt. "I hope you know that this wasn't really my plan." He held her ass, pulling her tighter against him. "I love the way your mind works, however."

"Ride me." Her blouse seemed to just disappear when he started pulling at it. Her breasts were bared, his mouth on them before she could catch her breath. When he bit down hard enough to make her cry out, he lifted his head and looked at her. "Strip. Now."

The command in his voice had her wet. When he pushed her to the other side and began tugging at her pants, she nearly begged him to take her right then. He wanted her to ride him, but his cock was freed and his fist holding himself gave her pause. The thought of sucking his cock made her mouth water.

Stripping down to her bare skin, she moved to sit on her knees between his legs and licked him from tip to groin. His precum tasted delicious, and she found she wanted that more than anything he was offering her. As soon as she took him into her mouth, he began fucking her hard, his hand curled to the back of her head to hold her.

Sending him images was something she'd wanted to do for a while now. Not just of the two of them, though that was erotic enough, but what she thought of when they had sex. Him coming over her. Mitch standing up, his cock stiff and oozing cum all over her while she sat there with her mouth open. Another image of what she thought he'd look like with her tied in front of him, her arms wide and her legs spread open. He was eating her, his hand digging so deeply into her ass that there would be marks. Her face covered in a mask so that when he did touch her, it would be a surprise to her.

"Christ, you're killing me." Looking up at him while she curled her tongue around his thick crown, she could see his eyes were hooded, his mouth slightly open. She wanted to watch him as he came down her throat, and needed to taste him this way. Reaching between his legs, she cupped his heavy balls in her hand and rolled them, watching his face to see if he enjoyed it. But when he stiffened, his hips lifted up off the seat, she tasted the first of his cum and slid her fingers into her pussy to come with him.

He cried out his release as he filled her. Swallowing as much as she could, licking her lips when drops of it slipped out, she nearly fell back when he pulled from her. But then she found herself on her back on the seat and him deep inside of her.

"Come for me. I want to feel you tighten around me again before I come again." Her legs wrapped around him, and his body, stiff and hard, pounded her harder than he'd ever done before. And when she pulled his throat to her mouth, she knew the exact moment when he came. Vinnie sank her teeth into his pounding pulse just as her world shattered with her own release.

She drank deeply of him. And even when he sat up, pulling her body with his, she didn't stop. He was hers, and even though it had only been a day since she'd seen him, Vinnie could not believe how much she'd missed him. When she had her fill, she sealed the wound and held him to her as she rested. His soft chuckle had her lifting her head to look at him.

"We're going to have to pay for the seats to be repaired, I think." She looked at where he had pointed and could see that they'd torn the soft leather. Laying her head back on his shoulder, she told him it was well worth it. "I love you."

"I love you as well." She moved off his lap and started to pull on her clothing. He, too, began to dress, but neither of them stopped touching the other. A kiss here, a brush of fingers there. It was soft and loving, and probably the best thing in the world to sooth her. "My father is calling for my death."

"I heard. Billy said you were really nervous about it." She nodded as she pulled on her shoes. "You don't have anything to worry about. I guess the council, the vampire council, is looking into his behavior. Steele said they wanted to meet with him, and he'd like for us to be there, as he knows little to nothing about your bylaws. But they're holding me to my promise to send him away. And I plan to as soon as I see him."

"I can go with Steele, that's no problem." She lay back on the seat and held his hand in hers. Vinnie didn't want to talk about her dad right now so changed the subject. "The inventory is done at the warehouses. Grandmother even had her things brought over. Everything is marked but not priced as yet. A guy that Connie knows is going to come and tell us what we should charge for each piece and the least we should take for it. I guess he worked in an antique shop until his death, and now he just hangs out in them. He has a lot of knowledge."

"Billy said you have the building ready to go too. That's working pretty well for them as well. He said you hired a bunch of the homeless at the shelter to work for you." She nodded, feeling slightly embarrassed. "Are any of them going to stick around and work after you get open?"

"A few of them. There are two men that seemed to be really excited about being the delivery men. Grandmother and I looked at moving trucks and we got a good deal on one to use. Hugh is helping them learn to drive it. They can both drive, but it's been a while, they said." He smiled at her. "I gave my notice at the firm too. I think they were sort of glad to get rid of me for some reason."

"I doubt that. From what I've heard about you — and yes, I did have you investigated — you're fucking amazing at your job." She nodded and leaned back when he did. "We'll have a grand opening when you're ready. Connie said she knows the best people to invite. I forgot to ask her if they were living or not. She's wonderful."

He fell asleep. They weren't far from their home, but she let him sleep. Billy had been coming to see her while Mitch and the others were gone to tell her how he'd helped the young man that had killed himself. And what had happened with the woman and man.

I need to talk to you. Now. Get your ass over to the place where you murdered me. Her father's voice rang in her head as if he were standing right next to her. And the anger in it made her smile. She had long since gotten over any kind of rules or commands that he could make her follow.

Did it ever occur to you that if you had treated me with anything but contempt or hatred that I might want to help you? He told her it was her duty. *No. It was your duty to be a parent I could depend on. You were never that, and neither was Mother.*

She was a good mother. And you never forget that. She never drowned you, did she? Or sold you off to those people willing to give us a lot of money. The things I could have done with that much money. But no, your grandmother said it wasn't right. I think not killing you when we had the chance made us wonderful parents, don't you? Vinnie was too shocked to answer him. *Now, get your ass over to the grounds that you killed me on. You're going to help me get myself back together. And you'll do it or so help me, Victoria, I will make you pay.*

How? Her father started to tell her how to get to him. *No. I know where I killed you. It's a place I go to often when I want to feel good about myself. How is it you think you'll make me pay? Do you think to come into my house and murder me? Won't work. We've taken precautions so you can't. Are you going to tell Mother to come to me? Won't work either. She's dead, thanks to the council. Who, by the way, said you should have been killed long before I volunteered for the job.*

You volunteered to kill me? What kind of child did we raise? You're not a child of mine as of this moment. She started to point out she'd not been a child to them since she'd taken her first breath, but he spoke before she could. *Now, get over here now, Victoria. It's your duty as my child to help me.*

You just disowned me. He said nothing. *No. I'm not going to you. I won't be bothered by you again. Don't contact me again, Father. Or so help me, I'll have Mitch come to you and zap you over right this minute. And so you know, he is coming for you.*

She closed the connection between them. It was much easier than she'd ever thought it would be. And she knew it was solid too, the wall she'd put between them. She wondered if it was because he'd told her she was no longer a child of his or something else that gave her the ability to cut him off. Not that it mattered, he was gone and she felt free of him.

When they arrived at their home, Vinnie woke Mitch up and he smiled at her. She thought it was the most precious thing in the world, to see him smiling at her with such love. She touched her fingers to his cheek, then to his lips. She smiled back at him when he bit her finger.

"I do so love you, Mitch. I don't know how I ever thought I could not have a mate." He kissed her fingers now and held them to his heart. "You are by and far the best thing that has ever happened to me, and will be forever."

"I want to have children with you." She nodded, her eyes filling with tears of joy. "I'm not sure how it works with me being human and all, but I'd very much like to have several children with you."

"It's the same way." He nodded, still smiling. "Our children could be necromancers or vampires, or a combination of both. Even just human. With the two of us being what we are, we can't know what our children will be."

"They're going to be loved, cared for, and will know we love them more than life itself." There was a knock at the window and they opened the door. Vinnie wasn't surprised to see her grandmother at the door waiting for them, but what she was surprised about was the fact that the council was standing on the wrap around porch.

"We'd like a word with you, if you please?" Nodding, Vinnie glanced at her grandmother, who was smiling. "There is a problem we'd like to talk over with you. It's about...well, not a problem but a...we were wondering that...should you like to —?"

"Could you just ask me?" She knew she should have curbed her temper a little, but they were making her nervous. "Just ask me or tell me whatever it is you're doing here."

"We have items too. That we'd like for you to sell for us. We've no desire for the money, should it sell, but we have so much...we'd like to rid ourselves of the burden of taking care of it."

Mitch laughed, and she had to think what they were saying. "You have items? As in old furniture?" The man nodded and smiled at her. "I don't understand. How is that a problem that...unless you mean there are more than just the three of you that have items you want to get rid of."

"There are many of us. We would like to have the things handled by you, as we have said, but we'd also like for you to take the money and put it into a fund to help others like us." She asked him what he meant. "There are so many of the older vampires that have lost so much. Due to poor planning or other reasons, there are many vampires that are without even the basic needs of a place to rest. These people are not like your parents. They are not as understanding in the world as we have become and have been taken advantage of."

"So you wish to sell your things in my shop so that you can fund these other vampires that have nothing. You can't do that." He asked her why. "Well, for one reason, I have to account for the money that I make. Secondly, if you put it out there that you'll be helping everyone with their hand out just because of poor planning, then you're going to have a bunch of people not doing shit, because why should they when you're giving it all to them? Then you'll have others coming around too. Humans that work for these vampires. They'll want their share of it as well."

"Yes, yes, I can see that." They were all nodding, and she thought of something else. "We would be overrun by anyone that thinks to be taking advantage of our funding."

"Who would run this foundation you're setting up?" They looked at each other, then at her. "Oh no. I'm not doing it. You're going to have to find someone else to do that part. I'll sell off your things if I can, but I'm not going to run that as well. I have a life. I want to have children, and I have a mate I'd like to see every once in a while."

"I would love to do it." They all turned to her grandmother when she spoke. "I've been trying to think of things to do. I have some friends I'd like to see, but more that I'd like to avoid. But I think this will be just what I need to...well, to feel like I'm productive again."

"Then it is settled. We will give you a list of the inventory we have acquired and get it to you within a fortnight. After that, we'll set up all accounts that are needed to make this work for all concerned."

As they moved away, talking to her grandmother, Vinnie looked at Mitch. He had the strangest smile on his face. She asked him what was so funny.

"I'm going to be married to a vampire who works for the council, who just happens to love me right back. Life couldn't be any better if we tried. Now if tomorrow goes well, we can get on with our lives." She hoped it would be that easy. But things had a way of fucking up. She knew this first hand.

Chapter 12

The courtroom was packed. Mitch looked around again and wondered why there were so many people there for this. He was both terrified and embarrassed by it all. When his attorney slapped him on the back and told him not to worry, his worry doubled. The guy was just entirely too chipper for his tastes. Mitch looked around the room again.

You're worrying too much. Mitch smiled at the sound of Vinnie's voice in his head. Last night they'd gotten a call that the hearing had been moved to later in the day, and she'd not been able to attend with him as he'd hoped. *I'm there with you, just not physically. What has you so worked up?*

There must be two hundred people in here, and I'm not kidding either. Then there are the ghosts. Some of them are sitting on the laps of the humans like they're the only ones here. It's almost comical. She laughed in his head and he felt better. *You did that on purpose, didn't you?*

Yes. You need to just relax. According to your attorney, this is a piece of cake. Though why he wants cake and not a thick juicy steak is beyond me. Mitch glanced over at the man they were talking about. He was a shifter, a wolf, and Mitch had to stifle a laugh when he grinned at him again. The man really was too happy all the time. *Just let it flow. If they win, which I highly doubt, then I will hunt them down and drain them for you. It would taste nasty being that they're who they are, but I'd do it all in the name of love.*

It took him several seconds to realize she was kidding. At least he hoped so. There were times when he was never sure. Like now. Was she or not? Either way, he didn't want to think about it right at the moment. When the judge was announced, everyone stood up and he felt his heart beat just a little harder. It was do or die time.

The other lawyer stood up to give his speech. Hell of a speech it was too. He went on about how the Bruces had been struggling for years, that they'd been having trouble feeling their confidence again after what had happened to them that horrid night. And how the government had treated them since, giving them little to no work. So little, in fact, that Mr. Bruce had had to take on a second job, one that took him out of the house when his wife of thirty years needed him the most.

Mitch's lawyer stood up, but instead of speaking, he turned to the back of the room. A single man stood up and asked to speak to the judge. As he made his way to the front of the room, several people started whispering, but the judge put an end to that quickly.

"There will be order in my courtroom." No one said another word and the man that had come from the back was standing in front of him. "Now, young man, I'm assuming you have something you'd like to say? And it had better be relevant, if you know what's good for you."

"Yes, sir. It's about this case. I know that before the lawyer for the defendant speaks I have to ask you if I may be represented by the same attorney. To save time." The judge looked at him, then back at the young man. "I should like to make it known that I was also abused by the Bruces, and barely made it out at all. I want to put in my two cents worth."

"Your honor. That isn't right. He'll have to file like the rest of us did." The judge leaned back in his chair and seemed to be thinking as Jefferies continued. "Besides, we can't repute his claim or his charges against this nice family."

"You saying you want to throw your hat in with this man? You know what will happen if he were to lose, don't you? You'd not be able to come back on him or the *nice* family over there." He made it sound as if he didn't believe they were any nicer than they were telling the truth. But the man, Donnie James, said he wasn't worried. Just as he sat down, handing a file to his attorney, another man stood up and asked the same thing.

After the third man stood up and was given permission to join Mitch's side of the table, the judge asked how many more there were that were going to come along for the ride. Roger, his own attorney, stood up and cleared his throat. The judge grinned, but Mitch was beginning to worry about this.

"In here, sir, there are nine more men." He asked him what he meant by in here. "There are about a dozen or so more out in the hall. There wasn't enough room for them all to come in, your honor."

"So you're saying that you now have over two dozen men that want to be a part of the suit against the Bruces in the same venue as this man here?" Roger nodded and asked to approach. "If you tell me that you're part of the alleged abuse, I'm going to be highly pissed off, just so you know."

"No, sir, I'm not. But I do have affidavits from each man, with dates and hospital records as well. They were nice enough to bring them with them today, as I had no knowledge of their coming forward." The judge just cocked a brow at him, but neither of them said more. As they stood there, staring at each other, Mitch looked over at the Bruces. He wondered how many others they might have abused in the name of whatever the fuck was going through their minds at the time.

They were squirming. Not only that, but arguing as well. Carol looked like she was telling her husband to go on with this, there was no way they could lose, but Mark was saying no way. Their attorney, Jefferies, put his hands on both their shoulders and told them to wait. The judge picked up his gavel when the room started to erupt in voices again.

"Now see here. You want me to clear this room?" No one answered him, and the room was suddenly quiet. "Good. I'd like as many people as we can get in here to see this. This is...this has got to be the worst case of work for the system as I have ever seen."

After turning to the bailiff and telling him to bring in the rest of the men, no one said a word, but Mitch was thinking this was going to be disastrous. As they came in, one by one handing a file to Roger, they lined up around the back of the room all the way to the front. There were more than five dozen men standing around the room.

"Your honor, I had no idea." The judge only nodded and asked to see the files. Making two trips to the dais, Roger gave the judge the files and then asked for them to wait. He had looked over a few of them when Jefferies finally spoke.

"Your honor?" The judge told him to wait. "Your honor, my client would like to see this trial ended. There is no proof whatsoever that what these men are claiming is even real."

"I'm thinking you might want to shut your trap and let me read here. And as for proof, I'm looking at some pretty damaging proof right here." The judge said a name, and the man stepped forward. "You claim that you have a video of the alleged rape from the Bruces. You have it here?"

"I do, your honor. I wasn't sure if it would help or not, but I did make a couple of copies. The night this was taken was...I was eleven, sir. And I had only been with them for a few days when I found this cell phone on one of my trips to the yard." He asked him what he meant by that. "Daily, sir, they would take us to the yard, hose us off, and give us a bottle of dish detergent. Then they'd hit us with the water to make it so that we'd be—"

"They were fucking nasty." When Mark stood up and screamed at the judge, no one made a sound, not even his lawyer. Mitch could hear Vinnie laughing in his head, but was too shocked to see what she thought was so funny. "Do you have any idea how smelly they were every day? There was no way I wanted them in my bathroom to piss, much less to shower."

"You made them do their business outside too?"

Before Jefferies could tell him to sit down and shut up, Mark answered the judge. "You bet I did. And they'd have taken their meals out there too if...if...." He seemed to have realized in that moment what he was saying. He paused long enough to let a mask—and that was what it looked like—seem to fade over his entire body. "I've been ill lately, dealing with all of this. You're going to have to forgive me of my ramblings. Sometimes I say things that aren't true. Like this."

"I'm betting that sort of thing goes over you all the time." Mark nodded, but Mitch was pretty sure he thought the judge was being sympathetic and not a smart ass. Yeah, he thought, you are a liar, that's for sure.

The judge and the man who had brought the video were taken to the back offices as the rest of them sat there. His lawyer, as well as the one for the Bruces, were asked to join them almost as soon as the door shut behind them. Mitch took the time to look around the room at the men seated now, thanks to the judge, and wondered about them.

Several of them were in suits. A few more were in only jeans and shirt, no tie or jacket. There were three that looked like they were dressed for something other than a courtroom, and more like they were headed to the gym afterwards. Each of them had a haunted look about them, and most of them were not looking in the direction of the Bruces. The few that were looked as if had they had a gun, both of the people who had cared for them would be dead.

Connie sat down next to him when he looked over at the couple as well. "They're not dealing with this well, are they?" She laughed her little laugh, and he had to smile. "I know you can't speak to me without having them look at you as if you'd gone over the edge, but I can tell you a bit about the men there. Not all of them, but some."

He looked at the man she pointed out. He appeared well-dressed if a little haggard. He was a large man, with big hands and chest. Not fat, but big all the same. He was one of the few that were glaring at the Bruces.

"When he was younger and living with those people, he vowed if he ever got out alive he'd make sure that no one had to go through what he had as a kid. His home has seen more than five dozen children go through there, and all of them still call him Dad and his wife Mom. They gave those children a chance at life as well as a hand up when they went to college. He has devoted his life to helping those who could not have made it without him." He wondered if there was a way he could help as well, and made a mental note to ask Vinnie what they could do. "The man sitting next to him has been helping the kids on the street. He's a surgeon. He and his office staff go to the streets twice a month to help those that need it. Kids that have nowhere to go and no one to turn to. He also has a friend who is a dentist that goes with him, and they offer free dental exams as well as any surgeries that need to be performed."

As she pointed out what each man was doing to come to terms with what had happened to him, he realized he'd done nothing. Not one thing to help those that might have been going through what he had. When he felt Vinnie's anger, he sat up higher in his chair and started to reach for her, but she was speaking before he realized her anger was at him, not something with her.

You dolt. Mitch might have laughed at the old word had he not been a little afraid she might have come to him and murdered him. *What do you think you do every single time you help one of the lost people? You think that had you been killed any night you were with those people that any of the ones that you help would have gotten your help? You think they would have been able to have closure or anything else they needed had you not been what you are? Or doing what you do for them?*

I'm pretty sure that Steele or any of the rest of them would have been able to — Vinnie told him to shut up and listen. He did, thinking she was kinda scary when she was pissed off.

Yeah, you think that that boy you just helped, you think that they could have done as good a job as you did? I don't. You could feel his pain because you'd lived it. You were able to be there for him as none of the rest of them could. He didn't say anything but listened to her now. *Those other boys you've helped. They needed you, not Steele. Though I think he's a good man, he doesn't have the kind of experience you have in dealing with those kinds of pain. You helped them because you knew what they were feeling.* She paused to take a breath, and he smiled. *But you and I can do much more than we are now. I think your idea of opening a shelter for them is great. I have just the building we can use, too. We can bring in more doctors and help. Offer some scholarships if they need it, along with some mental health counselling.*

I think that's a wonderful idea. He looked around the room, seeing the people for what they were. Men who had not just risen above what had happened to them, but also had gone on to make sure things were better for those that followed. And so had he in a different sort of way. Ten minutes later the Bruces were asked to join them in the chambers, and Mitch started to get nervous.

When the judge and the two lawyers come out of the chambers, he waited for the Bruces, but they never came out. When the judge started talking, it was all Mitch could do not to jump up and down, laughing.

"The Bruces, after much...discussion, have decided to drop their suit against the forenamed people. They instead are being brought up on other charges." No one said a word for several seconds, waiting like him, he was sure, for there to be some sort of explanation. When it came, it wasn't from the judge. It was from Billy.

"They're going to jail." Mitch looked at the older ghost. "And let me tell you, they won't last all that long there either. We got us some people they have hurt going there to talk to them a little. You might say they're going to be judged by a different kind of jury. And they've been found guilty already."

They were making their way out of the courthouse some twenty minutes later when the first of several of the other men approached Mitch about what he'd done, and to tell him thanks. Mitch had never been so grateful for the support of his friends and family than he was in that moment.

~~~

The doors to Old Things opened two days later. The huge warehouse was filled from top to bottom with not just antiques, which took up most of the five stories, but also newer items such as drapes and fixtures. There was a line outside the building when Vinnie left to go home to rest. Nine people were working today, on this special day, and she wondered if there would be enough help. Addie and Kari were just getting out of their cars when Vinnie locked the back door.

"We've come to help out. And it looks like you can use us, too." Vinnie watched them move to the front of the store, and she called them back. Handing them her keys, she told them where to find the person in charge.

"She's not very confident in herself, so I would expect to have her ask lots of questions. There are others that can work the job, but she's the one that said she can do this. I think she can as well, but...." Vinnie shrugged. "You really don't mind helping out? Oh, and Max is in there too. He's a ghost that will be helping you with prices, as well as whatever questions the people might have on a certain piece."

"We're excited." Vinnie looked at Kari's belly, envying her having a child by the man that she loved. Soon, she told herself. Soon she and Mitch would have children as well. Addie looked at her and smiled. "You'll be here soon enough."

"I hope so." Kari nodded. "We're just talking. I don't know...we're trying to figure out a lot of things right now."

"So are we." Vinnie looked up at the sun. "You'd better get going. I know how to get in touch with Mitch if we have any problems, and he said he could contact you too. It'll be fine, you'll see."

Moving her body, running down now with the sun so high in the sky, she made her way to her lair. As she moved into the room, she felt the weight of the sun taking her nearly to the floor. She knew she was going to have to rest more than she had lately, and blamed it on the stress of the new store. As soon as her head hit her pillow, she was out.

Waking, she nearly screamed when she felt someone in the room with her. She tried to peer into the darkness. It frightened her on so many levels to know someone had gotten into her rooms with her when she'd been sleeping. When a light flared, she sat very still on the side of the bed and looked at the man in front of her.

"Hello. In the event you don't know it, I'm not here. Or there. Whatever you want to call it. I'm at my home, and you are there." Nodding, she stood up, glad now that she'd been too tired to undress before sleeping. "I need your help."

"I'm not the police." He laughed, and she moved to turn on the lights. With the light on, it seemed less creepy to have him in her room. "You need help, perhaps you should go to them."

"But it's my daughter. She's not dead, but I can't seem to locate her at all. It's like she has fallen off the face of the earth." She asked him what he meant. "Dillon, my daughter, is human, but...she has some abilities that make her a commodity to others. She can find things that are thought to be lost."

"You mean she uses psychometrics." The man smiled and nodded. "You could have just said that. Told me what she can do."

"Most would call her a fake, a token or object reader. I know what she can do. I've seen it. And not just with things either, but with people as well. She's found...there was a missing child, and Dillon was able to find her." She asked him where she was. "Ah, there lies the ten million dollar question. I don't know. I can usually...well, contact her through a link that we share. Most of the time, there is just the two of us working this thing. I can find things as well, you see, but not like she can. She is brilliant at it. But as of a few weeks ago, I have not been able to reach out to her at all. It's like I'm hitting a wall."

"And you know that she's not been killed." He nodded. "And how do you know this? I mean, for sure. Could there just be nothing there because she's gone to you? I don't mean to be cruel, but I'm trying to understand this."

"I appreciate your questions. I've asked myself the same ones over and over. If she's gone, then why has she not contacted me? Or one of you? It's...we have both said that should either of us die, then we were to contact Steele Bennett or one of his men. As far as I know, she has not." That was a good way to know but not foolproof. "And there is this."

He held up an envelope, and she walked to it to see if she could make it out. But it was too dark where he was, and she just saw it had a name on it. Dillon Malone. He moved it when she asked him to, and then she could see it did indeed say that name.

"Is this her or you?" He laughed. "Yeah, that's not a traditional girl's name, so I thought I'd check. Who are you by the way? And why have you come to me?"

"Her name is Dillon, as is mine, but I go by my last name. I have since I was a youngster. She's my onlyest." Vinnie nodded and sat back in her chair as he continued. "I got this letter yesterday. And it said I was to contact you if I was going to get any real results. The rest of the people in the business will help, but this note said I was to have you help me. I don't know why, unless you do."

"I don't know anything about any of this." She watched the man as he paced on his end. He seemed to be talking to someone, and she reached for Mitch to let him know what was going on. *He said his daughter is alive. How do I find out if she's alive or not without running into her?*

I'll ask Billy or Connie to look. Aster can too. She is having fun at the shop, by the way. I guess her and the man that is helping you out are getting along really well too. Oh, and you should know that you've sold some really big pieces today. I don't know which ones, but...we're kinda busy here. She asked him where he was. *Right now we're in an old court house. I mean really old. There are some clients here that have been here since the turn of the century. Hang on, love, Aster is here now. Let me ask her.*

"I'm going to send you a copy of this letter I have." She looked at Malone and he showed her the letter, but she couldn't read it any better than she could the envelope. "Do you have a fax machine there?"

After giving him the number, she moved out of her rooms into the hall. Hugo was there as well as Gilda, like they were every night when she rose. She was being updated on things from Gilda as they entered the office. She pulled the letter off just as Gilda left her with the phone messages she had. As she read over the file, she felt her world sort of tilt. She wasn't just supposed to find this girl, but she was to keep her safe as well.

"Do you know what it means?" She told Malone that she didn't. "Neither do I. Why does whoever wrote that think you can protect her any more than I can?"

"I don't know. But you said she's human. And that you are as well." He nodded. "Don't lie to me, Malone. I'm not in the mood to be fucked with here."

Aster said she's not dead. Being held, but not dead. Mitch paused before continuing. *What's going on?*

I don't know just yet. He told her to get back to him if she needed him. *Always. I will always need you. But her father is lying to me. I'm not sure why, but he is.*

"She's not human. I am, but she's not." He sat down and looked to her like he was floating on air. "She's not my daughter either. Not of my blood anyway. She is, however, something special. And as for me lying to you, it's all I've done to keep her safe since I found her on my front porch. She can find people and things, as can I, but she's so much stronger than me. I just want her home and safe."

"And this letter, it's real?" He told her it was. "All right. She's not dead. A friend of mine looked around and she's not dead. But you lie to me again and I will drain you. You do understand that, don't you?"

"I do, and I won't. I just need her to come home to me."

Vinnie glanced at the letter she had in front of her after Malone left her. It said that he was to contact Victoria Riley. Not Vinnie Graham, but Riley. And he was to tell her everything that was listed on this letter.

No police. No Feds, and absolutely no weapons at all were to ever be on her person when she came to talk to them. Whoever they were, they expected her to be easy.

"Fuck that shit." She grinned at Hugo when he tisked at her. "Hugo, my dear friend, we might just get ourselves in trouble over this one."

"That will be a change how, my lady?" She laughed at his seriousness and decided it was time to go see how the store was doing. Closing time was in an hour, and Vinnie needed to think too. Going out into the night, she told Mitch what she knew and what the letter had said.

Don't go there, wherever they want you to meet them, without someone with you. She told him she'd take her Hugo. *I like that idea. He's nothing but a big old cat, and no one will notice that he's a shifter too.*

Before long, she knew she'd have to find someone to watch over Mitch as well. Hugo was her helper, and even though Mitch was her mate, she couldn't watch over him all the time. Putting that on her list of things to do, she entered the store. Vinnie had a lot of things to do there before the sun came up in the morning.

Now Available in the
Justice Series

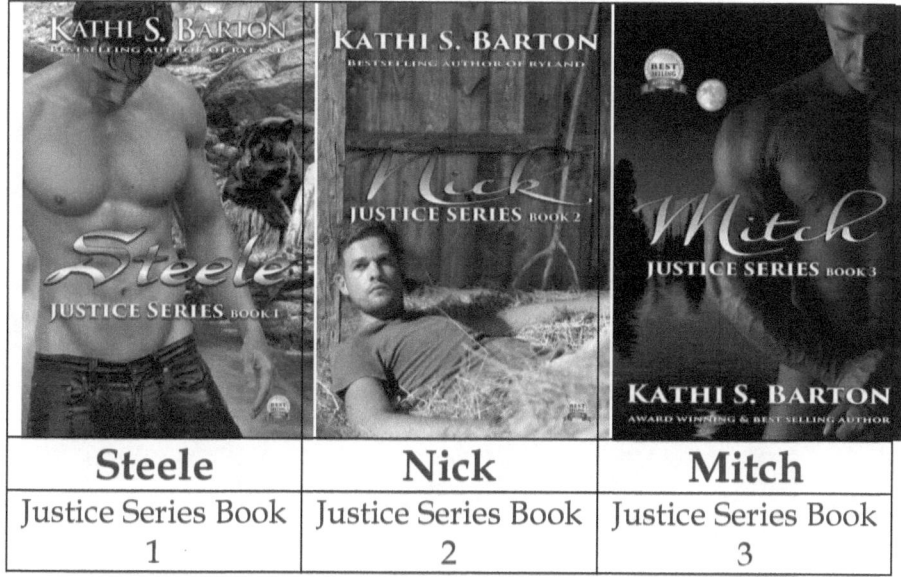

Steele	Nick	Mitch
Justice Series Book 1	Justice Series Book 2	Justice Series Book 3

Before You Go...

HELP AN AUTHOR

write a review

THANK YOU!

Share your voice and help guide other readers to these wonderful books. Even if it's only a line or two your reviews help readers discover the author's books so they can continue creating stories that you'll love. Login to your favorite retailer and leave a review. Thank you.

AWARD WINNING, BESTSELLING AUTHOR

Kathi Barton, author of the bestselling series Force of Nature, lives in Nashport, Ohio with her husband Paul. In addition to writing full time Kathi likes to spend time with her eight grandkids, three children and three children-in-laws. She writes to relax and have fun.

Her muse, a cross between Jimmy Stewart and Hugh Jackman brings them to life for her readers in a way that has them coming back time and again for more. Her favorite genre is paranormal romance with a great deal of spice. You can visit Kathi on line and drop her an email if you'd like. She loves hearing from her fans. aaronskiss@gmail.com.

Follow Kathi on her blog:
http://kathisbartonauthor.blogspot.com/